That Makes Sense

The Onsite Chronicles

Sandeep Pawar

ukiyoto®

Ukiyoto Publishing

My father, Dr. M. S. Pawar, would have been so proud of me.

Baba, I miss you. I know your blessings are always with me.

Acknowledgements

First of all, I would like to thank and bow to Indian and British Gods for their everlasting blessings on me. Beside that community, I thank all the people who knowingly or unknowingly helped me to climb the corporate ladder and achieve the most dreamed dream-the onsite opportunity.

I express my deepest gratitude towards my family for giving me enough time to complete this book and minimally ordering me for completing other household work.

I am particularly grateful to Suyog Upadhye for his valuable comments on the storyline and structuring it.

My heartiest thanks to Sangeeth Sankar who designed the beautiful cover accommodating my little tantrums. Because of such a pretty cover, I sometimes wish-people should judge the book by its cover. I also thank Sameer Rana for clicking my photo which I use as an author picture everywhere. He not only clicked it but shared it with me on time.

I also thank numerous friends who supported my writing and also promised me that they'll buy and promote the book. Let's see whether they keep their promise and thus the friendship goals alive.

And you readers, I sincerely thank you for picking up this book and I hope you will be entertained till the last word. Sit tight and enjoy the ride.

CONTENTS

I, IT and IIT

One monotonous morning with sleepy eyes when I was slurping my machine-made coffee, my desk phone rang. The display informed it was from the HR department. Why was she calling? My heart skipped a beat thinking of a possibility of my HRA receipts turning out to be fake and in turn getting me sacked from my job. After 2-3 rings when my neighbour looked at the phone angrily, I picked it up and answered in the most innocent way possible,

"Hello?"

"Hey, good morning! A quick question - Do you have a passport?" Asked the voice at the other end. It was Ms. Mousami, the HR. My heart skipped a beat again. Was that foreign calling? Was I so lucky? The best question any HR could ask you is, 'Do you have a passport?' Provided that is not just for records.

Her voice never felt so soft and silky. I had butterflies roaring in my stomach. My blood pressure shot up and made me dumber in excitement making me numb to react. Still, with shaking hands and trembling voice, I responded-

"Yes, of course. It's brand new and so fresh that it smells really good."

"That's great then. Let's meet after an hour. There is lovely news waiting for you. See you."

I stood still and stiff. Those thirty-seconds had turned a monotonous morning into a delightful one. I felt like a winner. Sleep in my eyes turned into a crazed thrill. Excitement can make you frozen and your hormones super-excited. I badly needed to rush to the toilet. I turned around. My neighbour was staring at me; a big question mark on his face. He must have overheard the conversation like I used to do his. I knew if I waited there one more minute, he would attack and interrogate me about the call. I knew the best way of defence is to attack. Before he could ask me anything, I asked him,

"Do you know what the biggest lie is?"

He still had that question mark on his face.

"That coffee can kill your sleep," I answered my question, fake-yawned and left for the toilet.

Later that evening, I was standing by the window, observing every movement across my company campus, savouring hot tea – alone.

The accomplishment of onsite opportunity was blowing my mind. All the things were looking beautiful. Even my taste buds were not complaining about the bland machine tea. I looked outside. A few employees were arriving at the office with dismal faces, while a few others were leaving with pleasant expressions. There, working in shifts was a norm like in many other industries. Usually the remote was with the foreign teams, and we Indians had to dance to their tunes in the form of work hours, shifts, and overall processes.

'Inter-week work shifts are acceptable, but you know, last week, they asked me to come the first three days in the night shift and the last two in the regular shift. Can you believe that I worked evening from 6 to 3, and then again morning 8 to 5 the very next day? Simply ridiculous.' I remembered my neighbour in Bangalore PG complaining over a Sunday lunch one afternoon. *'And how can they expect us to eat rice three times a day?'* His angry voice was as hard as the rice on his plate.

'If you consider the number of people associated with the software industry in India, it is not an exaggeration to treat it as a religion. And just like any other religion, this too has devotees, fanatics, critics, entertainment, and ironies. The fact is, in India, the software industry is for all. This religion allows all to be its adherents.'

The rush of employees to catch their respective cabs and buses made me philosophical. Why do we work so hard? Why does man choose to have such a routine life? In India, the majority of people, especially engineers, enter this field because everyone else is. *'Sometimes, we can't restrict ourselves from committing the same mistake twice. Despite knowing it's a mistake, we fall into it. Science followed by engineering is one such example.'* I remembered one motivational speaker, who left his engineering midway, addressing budding engineers in an Engineering Institute.

Posh offices, delightful infrastructure, and delusive onsite opportunities attract most of the youth like me to the industry. While the first two are invariably true, the last one is doubtful and tricky. I urged my mind not to have such thoughts. This was not the time to be a philosopher and ignore the worldly pleasures waiting for me. But these random thoughts were not ready to leave me alone. A plethora of thoughts - my observations, friends' advice and discussions - funny and ugly, real and exaggerated, irrelevant yet meaningful, continued.

By the time I finished the tea, my mind had played a movie of my past, my present and the future in store. The movie of all random, disorganised and arbitrary elements!

If you ask me what the best example of a context switcher is, I would say human mind without any doubt.

With my ample experience in the industry, I know its perks and pitfalls. With rigorous experiences of friends and colleagues combined, I know the industry inside out. And I'm overconfident to think I know everything.

"Wait. Aren't colleagues your friends?" My neighbour shrugged.

"I will tell you another office-hack. Colleagues can never be true friends." My experience spoke. "And if they show they are, they are wearing a mask." I stated.

The neighbour looked at me hard. His expressions and gestures were enough to show his disappointment and disagreement.

"Well, but there are always exceptions. Like us." I acquiesced.

His expressions changed a little and he gave a shy smile.

There was a business card lying on one of the tables. I picked it up. Tea in one hand, and card in the other, I looked at it.

"*Suhas Sharma, Software Developer*" was written on it . I knew Suhas. I knew what Suhas's work was. I laughed at myself. Filling excel sheets was definitely not development. But, there was a pride in calling themselves developers. I never saw any tester's business card. Maybe, because they didn't want anyone to know they're testers. Every software person wants to be a *Developer,* and not a *Tester* before even knowing the actual roles of both. I have a recruiter friend who shared his experience once. He asked one candidate while interviewing-

"Can you tell me more about black box testing?" Surprisingly, interviewee replied,

"No Sir. I did not pay much attention to testing as I'm interested only and only in development from the beginning."

Someone saying, 'I want to pursue my career in testing' is like opting to bowl after winning the toss in *gully* cricket. You cannot hide certain lies. And the preference for testing over development is one such lie.

"Do you know what's ridiculous about IT?" My senior asked.

"Designations." He answered before I could part my lips. "If your designation says you're a developer that does not mean you will write codes. The designations in this industry are quite absurd and deceptive. You may get the title that you too don't understand sometimes considering the actual work you are assigned." He bashed ferociously.

Not surprisingly, he was trapped in QA when recruited as a developer.

"It's all politics. Dirty politics." He used to say. Politics is everywhere, no denial to that. IT industry is no exception. But it's sophisticated politics which peaks only during appraisal and promotion cycles. Those who don't get the promotion or expected appraisal rating consider themselves a victim of office politics.

'Our management sucks big time. The office politics is on the rise, and as I don't entrap my manager, I'm always down sided and ignored for promotion.' said my school classmate who was in group-news for successive promotions, and claimed it solely on her skills and secular management a year before.

The generality of IT professionals assert that there is nothing good in IT after a particular experience, but they don't leave this field. I can spot one out of three who advise- 'Leave the job. At least open a startup. Follow your passion.' when they are the ones who stick to the industry for a long time and whine about it all the time. But, I don't blame them. Every industry has imposters.

Startup is the new cool of this generation. Startup ideas, even though as hopeless as machine coffee, haunt these professionals, but the lack of courage and load of responsibilities makes them turn a blind eye towards those ideas and sob about them from time to time. Startups are so common that if you get an idea, there is always a startup working on it.

"For every unnecessary, there are startups. You think about a petty problem, and there is a startup giving you a sophisticated, costly, and unnecessary solution. Right now, the only startup which is missing is where someone comes and wipe your ass." My frustrated ex-colleague said after successive failures of getting a job in startups.

I spotted Arun, a victim of premature hair loss, walking hastily to catch the cab. He works in the finance section and deals with salaries. I haven't interacted with him often, but I remember his exact words during our orientation.

"You earn, you spend. People get uneasy not because of their unwise spending of money, but when they don't get where their money's gone. For that we keep records. But what if you have every record in your hand, and still you don't understand anything, how do you feel? Welcome, and ask our software folks about it. Ask them what haunts them? And they will shout in unison, 'salary slips'. In IT, very few understand their salary slip completely. Possibly, you can understand a girl completely, but not your salary slip."

The complexity in understanding our payslips gave birth to the term 'In-hand'. In-laws don't trust CTCs, neither do we; they want your 'in-hand' to decide whether to let your two hands become four.

Suddenly, there comes Ashish Kumar in the pantry. We exchanged smiles. He looked happy. He looked energetic. He was in a hurry to leave. Ashish had an arranged marriage recently. He once shared his arranged marriage journey, still clear to me.

There is a whole different level of respect for onsite grooms. No girl is recorded to have declined an initial meeting with an onsite boy. This also triggers the wish of unmarried engineers to go on overseas assignments to make a strong impact on the matrimonial site. Young bachelors seeking a girl for marriage also reported that the match rate and response rate from the girl shot up drastically after adding the current location outside India. This huge craze of going abroad does not stop only till Facebook and matrimonial sites. I've even witnessed a wedding card mentioning the groom went onsite two times to different locations in the details. Even there is a hidden ranking about the onsite locations where US tops, followed by the UK, and then the rest of the world. I have a friend who was posted to South Africa for a year and was mocked in a friend circle in disbelief that South Africa can have software companies. My other friend works with Dhaka Stock Exchange and he says he goes to Kolkata instead of Dhaka to avoid the embarrassment.

'The moment you complete your probation in the industry, you must target to fly abroad on the company's money,' the rough book of opportunist software engineer says. It further continues, *'the most humiliating experience in a reunion party for an IT person is, revealing several years of service with no onsite experience.'*

People say, asking a woman her age and a man his salary is an unofficial offence in India except in an arranged marriage where this is the first and foremost step. Also, there should be one more thing for IT folks, which is, asking about the onsite opportunities. It is disheartening to say, none and giving excuses of working in a product company and thus, not requiring support onsite.

I went to the washroom after finishing my tea with an endless train of thought. I splashed some water and reconfirmed that it wasn't a dream. While I was scanning my confident and happy face in the mirror, I noticed my hoodie, my IIT hoodie. Nearly a year has passed, but I was reluctant to give away my IIT merchandise. My friends feel that's how I boast. I ignore them. I know that's the thing I feel confident with. That's the thing I am proud of. And in the end, that's important. IIT is my first love.

IITs are the premium institutes of the country which are popular for the toughest entrance exams, huge government funds, overflowing facilities, fat salary job offers, screwed sex-ratio, foreign internships, misuse of taxpayers' money, and suicides. IT and IITs have a special bond in India. Software engineers settling abroad and IITians have so much in common. Few accuse them of being synonyms. I proved them right marginally.

There is no denying that IITians are blessed with the 'IIT' tag which accords them the surprising wonders and illogical favours like the preference for foreign visits. One friend wearing IIT Bombay hoodie went to his previous institution and was given royal treatment. Not because of his academic excellence, but due to the lotus in the IIT tag, and imagining him as a political hero.

But even with these presumptions, getting an onsite opportunity is not a cakewalk for IITians. They too need to try hard for that - they need to cajole the manager, boast the skills, and remind the people that they are IITians from time to time by some way or the other. Working in the software industry was renowned and well-respected a decade back, but now, the reputation of IT is declining. Aren't IITs and ITs sailing in the same boat?

Hoping your son makes it to the real IIT and daughter into the medicine is stereotypical for an Indian father. But, harbouring and nourishing a dream of going onsite abroad is not at all stereotypical for an Indian software engineer. Everyone loves to fly and explore other nations.

However, the happiness of going abroad on your employer's money is unmatched. For that matter, all materialistic pleasures on someone else's money are always amusing in the first place. Who doesn't love freebies?

Foreign onsite is not just fun and the easiest way of money making, it is a prestige amidst your social circle. There is no denying that these foreign opportunities are the main traits of the IT industries, and everyone strives hard to seize them. Few turn out to be lucky early in their career, and few keep on switching jobs to get lucky somehow someday. By working in the industry and becoming successful in the fundamental purpose of going onsite, I can say that, it is better to be smart and lucky than to be hardworking and intelligent. Getting the onsite opportunity is a matter of your luck, your relationship with the manager, relationship of your colleagues with their managers, project requirements, and at last your skill set. So, you must know where to work upon and their priorities to snatch this opportunity.

"What's the real IIT you talk about anyway?" One of my friends asked me politely when I was distributing my unsolicited observations and findings.

"Well, in the era when the Government decided to have almost an IIT per district or two, the pure old IITs I refer to the real ones."

"What crap!" he nodded in denial.

Subbu crossed my way while returning from the washroom. If you ask me to name three unlucky souls, I will rank Subbu somewhere. He was selected for the US onsite a few months back. He had everything, except one thing — the passport. His dreams were shattered when he revealed about it. So, the first thing you should pour all your efforts into is get a passport before entering the software field. If you already have, well, you are smart, positive, and optimistic. Even though you are so sure about your capabilities, skills and intelligence, you never know what's in the mind of God and the manager, and you could be the lucky one, so, get the passport as quickly as possible.

I don't understand why we, Indians, are afraid of getting the most important document. This whole passport thing has ruined several abroad dreams. What can be the most dreadful feeling of being selected for an onsite opportunity, but having no passport? Presence of mind is the most important advantage a person can have. One of my friends was asked about his passport, and the very moment he thought, 'Is that an abroad call? But what if I tell them the truth. I don't have a passport? Will they ask my colleagues to go and not me? Should I lie to them and see if God is with me?' He lied and fortunately, God was with him. He applied immediately and got a brand new Tatkal Passport within a stipulated time. Another not so God-friendly friend had to postpone his MS dreams for not getting a passport until his

GRE morning. That's why don't mess with Gods in India.

The main hurdle in getting the passport is bribing the policeman. Few smart-asses came up with this trick of taking an empty pocket to the police station during the enquiry and thus saved few hundreds, while few strive hard to get the passport during their student phase in the hope that students are less demanding. A friend of mine advised me to dress improperly.

"You must look poor. Get your old dress, and then face the policeman. Convince them you want a passport not for travelling abroad, but for a few academic formalities."

Another one advised, "Wear spectacles when you encounter the police enquiry."

"Why?" I exploded listening to the bizarre proposition.

"No, just wear. And if you don't have one, take mine."

"But why?"

"Have you ever seen a spectacled terrorist?"

***

On that momentous day when surprisingly HR bombed the great news, I couldn't pace up with excitement. I went to the toilet consecutively. In all those times, I spotted a nervous Gowardhan. I felt suspicious. His face was as agitated as mine.

"Hey, HR called you too?" I made a move.

"Yes, did she call you too?" Gowardhan's eyes came out and now hung beside his short nose.

"Yes, so what do you think I am diabetic to come here thrice?"

Was this destiny to have us together for this important phase of our lives again?

There is a unique bond between Gowardhan and me. We spent our college days together. We were roommates. We were classmates. More than that, now we are colleagues. The same companies rejected us and the same company selected us.

I haven't come across such a haphazard character ever.

Gowardhan and I were shortlisted for Singapore based-firm for the interview while in IIT. I went first. The interviewer asked a few alien questions. I was sure I wouldn't make it, and damn sure Gowardhan also would not. That much I knew him. As soon as this dude entered, interviewer asked an icebreaker,

"Havyomeyofren?"

Gowardhan did not understand and asked him to repeat. He repeated twice.

"Havyomeyofren?"

"So, what did you answer, and what was he asking?" I asked Gowardhan later.

I said, "Yes Sir, this is my first interview."

"Then?"

"And then he repeated his question, a little slower. He was asking, 'Have you met your friend?'."

From that point on, Gowardhan started movie-marathons to compete with the accent. He seemed on the right path until one day when we raided his room on an unusual hour to find out the movie-marathon of Transformers running in Hindi.

Gowardhan is fond of jokes and often throws them at the wrong times and wrong places. He is a self-proclaimed comedian.

"He is the Steve Jobs of jokes." His neighbour complained.

"Why?" I asked surprisingly.

"He overhears the conversation, steals the jokes, and calls it his own."

One afternoon, during the lunch in the hostel mess, Gowardhan shouted,

"Hey, you know who is most manly in our mess?" And before anyone can think of any silly answer, he shouted, "Arey, it's *Dahi*. Wondering why? Because it's The HE".

"I told him this yesterday." The same neighbour whispered to me.

Varma was another colleague who was among the onsite troop. Varma was called dearly as FF, Fact Factory, as his fact knowledge was praiseworthy. He was senior to us, and his selection was no surprise. There was a rumour that Varma had joined the company on the only condition of working foreign onshore in near time, so there was no way out for the company to break the promise. Even after promising an instant onsite opportunity, he was forced to wait a year and a half. Onsite was not new to him.

We had heard enough of his Hong Kong visit. The information was also that he was sent to some African country for the office set up by his previous employer, but he never mentioned that. Varma always wanted to settle abroad, and he was trying hard for that. He has reportedly asked to shift him to the foreign office, but he was seduced with the sugar coated words. Gowardhan and I never had a healthy colleagueship with him. He seemed frustrated all the time. He used to rant about the frivolous issues, and so we never dared to go and converse with him. Also for us, 'two is a company, three is the crowd.'

"Varma is jealous of us," Gowardhan reported one day in the toilet, standing two urinals away from me.

"Why so, and who told you?" I suspected in a lower voice.

"Sources. And I guess only because he thinks IITians are overrated, over-packaged, and over-smart. One day, I heard him commenting - 'IITs are like a clan, you just need to get born there, and whoa, everything is sorted out for you in life.' Grapes are sour for him. He is not even an Engineer. I even have information where he said - he wondered how the management was sending us two newbies." Gowardhan continued in a voice like a foghorn.

"First, lower your volume. You remind me of those old factories with a buzzer for a lunch break. And second - that's none of our business. Let him spread anything and think as he likes. We are going to London, and that's it. And wait, isn't he an engineer?"

"No. He is some MC, BC."

"What?"

"Some MCA or BCA I guess."

"Ohh,"

"But don't forget he is accompanying us." Gowardhan listened to my advice and started advising me in a low pitch.

"We are two; he is one. Forget it." I gave a bottom line and left the loo like a boss. "And from the next time, we'll go outside and have this conversation. Loo walls are all ears." Boss in me ordered.

Mr Sitharaman, a newly married man in his early thirties, was the last one from the fantastic four gang selected for onsite. He was a technical lead and senior-most among us. The work pressure was visible in his eyes and its effects on his head. Due to his sparse hair and bald patches, he looked older, and that further triggered the poor man's stress level, trapping him in a vicious circle. He had already been to the UK before.

His suggestion I aptly remember-

"Take minimum luggage so that we can come back with maximum luggage."

What a wise man!

***

What the first and foremost unwritten rule before the plane takes off, is not to disclose the details of your onsite success with anyone in the office and home and in the world for that matter, to be on the safer side. The reasons are many. First, and the foremost is if you do not hold the passport and plan on getting the one immediately after the opportunity comes to you, your jealous colleague can bring this information to your HR, and your dreams could be shattered. Next one is this news can bring sudden disappointment among your competing peers, and more disappointment on your senior and more eligible peers. You are in this world to spread happiness, not disappointment and hatred. As soon as people get to know about the news, their perception towards you change. People start to behave nicely with you in the hope that you'll bring something for them in return. Your jokes get good responses. You get more emojis on your posts and more pings on the office messenger. Often, this fake behaviour turns you off. Most importantly, announcing this fabulous news is a strict no-no if any of your jealous colleagues know the *black-magic.*

'Don't count chickens before they hatch,' a famous proverb is not just for the sake of saying something.

As soon as I realised these detriments, I immediately got up from my seat to reach Gowardhan and warned him not to reveal anything until further confirmation. But that was too late for me. In between, Gowardhan's neighbour Harshwardhan congratulated with a big grin on his face,

"We are so happy that one of us got this chance." Harshwardhan was a part-time theatre performer. He was damn good at acting. I confirmed at the exact moment.

***

Watching clouds and a different soil through the aeroplane window and dreaming about the dream city which was a few hours away, I got a soft sleep. My dream was broken with a sound, unusual sound. The sound, maybe, I heard for the very first time in reality. I opened my eyes. I looked beside – Gowardhan's eyes wide open. I looked where he was looking. A young white couple sitting on the immediate front row was kissing. The sound generated by their activity was enough to disturb my dreams. How can a few people be so insensitive about other's dreams while enjoying theirs?

The couple then stood up. Hugged tightly and sat down. A minute later, the guy went in the direction of the loo followed by the girl. The kissing scene was still in my mind. I knew the UK had so much to offer in that context. Happy days were ahead. The clouds looked romantic. I went into my dream mode again. When I was about to close the eyes and take a nap, Gowardhan tapped my shoulder.

"Don't you feel the vibrations? Turbulence, turbulence" he said, winking continuously looking at the empty seats of the couple.

House away from home

"Get the damn keys, and let's get inside. It's freaking cold here." Gowardhan uttered, but was unable to produce enough voice due to frosty weather.

Everyone started looking at each other. Irresponsibility was visible in everyone's eyes. I understood. I made a move. Somebody had to. It was better to move than to freeze.

"Wait? Who has the keys? Get on the call with the owner."

Getting a house for rent in London is not a tough task if you are ready to spend a lot of money. You throw money; they will throw the amenities. Our company arranged the house for us and, of course, the colossal rent of that. When we reached London, we commenced to the house directly. The company arranged a taxi. The driver who was not looking like a driver from any angle from Indian perspective was standing at the arrival counter at Heathrow airport. 'Mr Sitharaman' reads his signboard. He was well suited.

"Welcome all of you. Let's get started." he welcomed.

"Shit! It's a BMW." Gowardhan was surprised.

"Don't get too excited. Don't let him know you've never been in a BMW." Varma instructed him brutally.

Mr Sitharaman out of courtesy asked the driver how much time would it take to reach.

"It usually takes 45 minutes, but fortunately traffic is less today, we should be good for 30 minutes." He replied softly. "And this is also showing 33 minutes. So, I'm not too wrong." He showed his GPS and tapped it in the way of saying, 'thank you' to the device.

Mr Sitharaman was in the front seat beside the driver. Gowardhan, Varma, and me in the middle. Varma was with headphones showing disinterest in the conversation.

The driver turned on the FM. Soothing music was running. Outside the window was another world I never imagined I could live in. London, the city of dreams. I was in my thoughts when someone tapped my shoulder,

"He doesn't look like British." Gowardhan was doubtful.

"Maybe. His accent is a little different." I affirmed.

"And colour too." He winked.

Breaking the silence, the driver asked, "Where are you guys from?"

"India."

"Oh, India. I know, I know. A lot of Indians here."

Indians are everywhere. Tons of them. Anywhere. Everywhere.

"Where are you from?" Mr Sitharaman asked.

"I'm from Congo. You know Congo?"

Mr Sitharaman turned silent. Maybe he is poor in geographics.

"Yes. In Africa, right?" But Gowardhan was not.

"Yes, yes. In Africa. Small country." The driver looked happy. The mention of motherland makes everyone happy. "You know, in London, you can find citizens of almost all the countries in the world. But as they are residing here for a long time, you can term them British." He continued.

We all agreed and confirmed that through our neck oscillations.

"Why are you here? To make money?" The driver had identified the real intention of the human species to come to London.

"Of course." Mr Sitharaman smiled.

"Yes, yes. Everyone is here to make money. I've been here since the last twenty years driving a taxi. A lot of money here." The driver laughed hard, after all, he was right in identifying our real intentions.

The addresses of the houses in London are quite short ones and seem very rich, like, 221 Bakers Street, 102 Richmond Road, and 501 Notting Hill. They are easy to find out. First of all because of the maps in smartphones, which everyone uses excessively, and the boards with the street names which are available at every corner, and essentially every house is labelled with a number.

"Here you are. Have a nice stay here." He stopped the car swiftly in front of a mansion which was going to be our house sooner. It took exactly 30 minutes as he initially suspected. Technology is subordinate, and intuition is fundamental.

Pulling out the luggage from the cab, we stood outside the big mansion in an extreme cold, which we never experienced in India.

Mr Sitharaman dialled the owner. On the call, the owner lady surprisingly asked, "Haven't you read the instructions I attached in the email?"

Have we read the attachment properly? We did not even open the attachment, forget reading it. In the attachment, with bountiful instructions about what not to do in the house, there were two significant things as well, the key password, and the WiFi password.

It was a big four bedroom mansion with a backyard garden. To our surprise, the description and the reality exactly matched - even the garden was precisely as shown in the picture. Otherwise, we also have swimming pools and play gardens in many of the new housing projects in India, but they won't tell us that those swimming pools will be water-less and gardens grass-free.

The house, four bedroom apartment, was too spacious for us. We were too tired to explore the entire house that evening, and went straight to sleep peacefully after an unpeaceful long flight journey on our randomised allotted separate bedrooms.

***

When you enter into the other culture, cultural shocks are expected, and so, they need not be perceived as 'shocks' because you must expect it.

The next morning, we all were excited for the first day at the office, but that all excitement was replaced by amazement when we realised there were three toilets, which was fine, but two of them were open commodes. Those commodes were inside the room beside the window just like a cupboard. First of its kind, the wall-less commode.

"Shit! What is this shit? Who will shit in this shit?" Gowardhan was shit surprised.

"That's why they say - it's an open culture." Mr Sitharaman jokes.

The western world is infamous for their tissue culture. We Indians love water on the other hand. This tissue-water rivalry crushes down Indians visiting western countries. So one of the most missed things in the foreign country is water, umm, not the drinking water per se.

The expected cultural shock you get is when you try to find a water tap or a jet after finishing your job in the toilet. Then you realise those white tissues kept are not only for wiping your hands. As a newbie, you are unsure how much you'll need. You try with two, considering the environment and the global warming warning at the bottom in the emails saying, *Save paper, save the environment.* But two are always insufficient. You snatch 7-8 more. You need to save yourself first, the environment later. What can happen just because of 7-8 more, eh? How much ice will melt because of your 7-8, eh?

We were disappointed. We were going to miss our regal Indian squat toilets. That was expected. We were prepared for that. But, open commodes? That was too much.

"Okay. Anyway, let's not make it an issue. We can share the one attached to my room." Mr Sitharaman suggested. He is a married man. Because of that, every problem looks trivial to him now.

"We all think Varma is sophisticated among us. Well, he is not." Gowardhan told me, holding a combo pack of toilet paper in a store.

"Ok. But why are you taking so many papers?" I expressed my concern over the pack sufficient for a year.

"You know what happened two days back?" He ignored my concern.

"No." Who says yes to such a question?

"I went to the toilet and after I was done, I searched for toilet papers but found none. Well, I couldn't go and get the toilet papers."

"Then?"

"Then I found the cardboard strap. You know that strap at the end of papers?"

"Then?" I knew where it would go.

"Then what? I tore apart half of that and served my purpose."

"But, how Varma becomes unsophisticated because you used cardboard?"

"Listen next. I knew the toilet papers were finished. I didn't tell anyone."

"Why?"

"I wanted all of you to suffer."

"Okay, then?"

"After a while, Varma went to the toilet. I knew he was in deep shit. He took a longer time than usual."

"You know his normal time as well?"

"I knew he was in the same dilemma as I was."

"Then?"

"Then what, he came out after a while. And I rushed to the toilet to see for any clues how he had escaped."

"And what did you find?"

"The remaining half of the cardboard vanished."

The house was equipped with all the appliances. You take the name, and that was there except for the pressure cooker.

"Mom, here we have everything, except - cooker." Rice-eater Gowardhan complained over the phone. A few seconds later, I heard him, saying, "No, no. That was not possible to carry here. Anyway, we will manage it. Don't worry."

There was a vast cutlery collection in the house - all sorts of forks, spoons, knives in all shapes and sizes one could imagine.

"Look at this monster." Gowardhan was holding the dangerous looking hefty knife.

"That's for chopping meat probably."

"I think they take a live animal home and cut it here with this." Gowardhan grinned.

For each damn activity, there was something, some appliance to assist you. The house had too much furniture to be a house.

"Even our furniture malls don't have this much," I mumbled.

Every room had an appropriate furniture structure like in a store. Every room was spacious except for the bathrooms.

"There is no mug here. And you know, they don't use buckets." Gowardhan resumed complaints over the phone.

"No, no. That was not possible to carry here. Anyway, we will manage it. Don't worry." He continued after listening to his mom's response.

The bathrooms were one of the cleanest places, but the bathing area was just too small.

There was a bathtub which we had only seen in movies and in soap advertisements where the fair girl always seduced us. In another bathroom, there was a glassy chamber like a captive place - a tiny one. Although they looked lavish, they were not suitable for Indian bathing style.

"Gowardhan, be careful. Don't break the glass while rubbing soap over the body. This place is tiny." Mr Sitharaman taunted.

"But I don't understand how these people take a bath daily. How do they apply soap?" Gowardhan was imagining.

"Have you seen soap anywhere here?" Varma appeared suddenly.

"No, but I have it. Do you want to?"

"Brits don't use soap. They have lotions. Look there. And, they don't take a bath daily. They take a shower."

"What's the big deal?"

"Shower is just with water. Bathing is with applying all the lotions and shampoos. In the tub. They are fair unlike us. They don't need to rub their skin daily." Varma had his homework done.

The bathroom which Mr Sitharaman suggested to share had a shower and a hand-shower. Hand-shower is their version of the bath mug we use in India. The commode was nearby. Gowardhan was facing a trivial problem in using tissues and was in search of innovative ideas. He then calculated the length of the pipe attached to the hand shower, and an idea trickled in his mind. The length was good enough to come to his rescue, and he did not mind using hand-shower as a multitasker. It could have been a secret unless he revealed his ingenious trick expecting praise for his innovation from us. He was, in fact, outraged and barred from entering that bathroom, and summoned to wash the hand shower for half an hour in the presence of someone from us.

"House numbers are mandatory to locate an address here. Look at the houses. They all are the same." I spoke about what I saw while walking in the lane.

"Yes. They are ditto. If you get the giant knife from our house and cut the two adjacent houses into four, you can exchange the parts. That won't affect. They are the same." Gowardhan retaliated.

House number was the only mark of identification. Without it, finding our house was not an easy job for us. In India, house numbers are mainly for couriers and postal. People describe their homes as - the yellow one, behind the banyan tree, home with a big tank on the terrace, and rarely mention the numbers to identify it for others.

Walking on the street was boring in London. What do you expect from empty roads with the same dead houses? But in India, it is the opposite. People try to be as different as possible than to their neighbours as far as their houses are concerned. There is always one or the other activity going on. You can notice someone young on the phone - some teen girl meandering in the balcony either playing with her hair. Or some young boy scratching his crotch. Or if not this, an open kitchen window and some cutlery noise coming out of it or a daily soap running on the television or a cricket match at a loud volume. The site is very lively on Indian roads occupied by distinct houses all around.

Housing services are very expensive in the western world, unlike in India. The middle-class Brits cannot afford such services, and need to do all such work by themselves. So, there is no *kaamwali bai* all the time for your service, and thus, I wonder what frivolous problems the homemaker women would be facing there. Because in India, more than anything, the root cause of daily problems revolve around this *kaamwali bai*. Their sudden and uninformed leave, which is practically always the case, boils the blood of Indian homemakers.

"That's the reason. That's why western countries are progressing." Gowardhan claimed.

"What's the reason?"

"Look. What's more frustrating for women? The irregularities of maids, house-workers, *kamwali* aunty. Isn't it? Here, there is no such scene. No house-worker, no tension, no stress. Perfect attitude towards development."

"Point." I appreciated it.

"See. As no one is looking interested to clean up the shared mess all over the house, I'm asking for house cleaning services. Our company would pay the bill. As they have paid for the huge rent, I don't think they'll mind for the services. All good?" Mr Sitharaman was the leader, and responsible.

As expected, an employee friendly company booked the service on a Sunday morning. Finding the house service is so easy in India. You need to go to the watchman and tell him there is a vacancy and you will be flooded with people willing to grab the vacancy. The only condition is you have to have good relations with the watchman.

London's case was different. Like all other

sophistications, this was also a sophisticated service. We got a mail confirming the service, the time, and the charge on per hour basis which we neglected out of habit.

"Listen. Install any split expense app. That's the most useful thing." Experienced Mr. Sitharaman paged.

There is a huge advantage to the people who can remember the shared expenses they paid and then purposefully forget the ones paid by others. The forgetful folks are often disadvantaged, academically of course and then in this way financially also. But the world is not of all bad people; there are a few demigods who want to serve these forgetful pupils. These good people came up with the technology to facilitate. They created simple mobile applications which keep a note of all the expenses and then announce at last, who owes to whom and how much. These apps allow us not to go face to face and inform others about the expenses you paid. Instead, you can silently insert all the small expenses which otherwise will break the relationship if directly asked. Sometimes, technology keeps the relationship going. However, my mother, like most of the other mothers, screams always that mobiles have ruined legitimate relationships and act as a catalyst for illegitimate ones. Duh!

Updating SplitApp became routine before sleeping.

"Take his more shares for toilet papers. Have you observed - he goes at least five times a day? I suspect something suspicious." Someone used to say jokingly. When we started sharing almost everything, everyone started eating like a bull. Who wants to contribute equally, but use less? SplitApp hiked my hunger which exercises couldn't.

Varma loved non-vegetarian food in London, and every other night, he used to bring something different and used to eat alone. One night, he came up with a Japanese chicken dish. He opened the box to see white curry inside. He was surprised. All other faces peeping in his box too were taken aback.

"Don't look at my food. Get yours. When are you dining?" Varma looked excited to try his Japanese dish and sat far away in one corner of the kitchen. We started roasting frozen *rotis*. After 5 minutes, he walked towards Gowardhan and asked-

"Hey, that was superb. I didn't predict the quantity. It's huge actually and I'm unable to finish it. Do you want to try the remaining? Otherwise, I need to trash it."

How could someone reject a tempting offer? Gowardhan agreed within a blink of an eye. "Yes, why not. Why trash when I'm here."

"Okay, that's on the table. Have it. Good night" Varma went to his room.

One bite of the chicken and Gowardhan howled-

"Eeeee! What choice Varma has!"

"Are you talking about the chicken or his colourful short?" I sincerely asked, remembering Varma's recent shopping.

"This food. Yaak! I'm going to throw this in the dustbin where it truly belongs to," said Gowardhan and stood up. His mobile beeped. He started towards the dustbin mumbling something. He stopped. He was checking something on his phone with bulged eyes in an unpleasant surprise.

"What happened?" I asked.

"Holy shit." He shouted. "You know that dickhead who just went to sleep, that jerk has split bill with me for this crap" he continued, looking at the poor white chicken.

Sunday, 10 AM.

The doorbell rang for the first time.

"This must be the house service." Mr Sitharaman walked up the door.

"Hello, Sir. Good morning." We heard a loud and clear feminine voice. Not wasting a moment, the rest of us quickly jumped in the hall to find the surprise in front of us.

A gorgeous girl in her mid-twenties was standing there. She was as white as curd. Her brown eyes with purple eyelashes were decorated with dark blue wayfarer spectacles. Her light burgundy hairs with two strips of red were open, but not messy. She had a backpack of Gucci. Her skin-tight navy blue jeans was perfect. On her jacket, it was printed Superdry. Her knee-length beige coloured boots looked clean and rich. She had an apple in one hand, not the fruit. She was a living kaleidoscope.

She handed over a few pages to Mr Sitharaman and asked - "Which way?"

"Oh, wow! If you have such ravishing beauty as a manager, who won't do over-time?" Gowardhan praised.

We were standing looking at her, her every action, her every expression, her every breath with our eyes wide open. Within a minute when Mr Sitharaman handed over the paper to her, she kept her bag on the table and removed her jacket. Our eyes stand still, happy and content. Why doesn't the world stop at such moments? Her white tight top was increasing the temperature. She was more than perfect.

"But wait. Why is she removing her jacket?" Gowardhan whispered, looking at the top.

"Do you have a problem?" I didn't want to restrict her.

"Because she is the one who will clean the mess." Mr Sitharaman explained.

"Is she going to clean? Is she a worker?"

"Yes. Seems so."

"I can't believe it."

"Neither can I."

"Oh God." Gowardhan was amazed to the greatest extent. The question 'How can such a beautiful girl be a cleaner?' was haunting him, and us too.

We postponed our plan of going out that day.

"Where can we get a better site than this?" Gowardhan winked.

She was a beauty with power. She cleaned all the mess in about three hours. She started packing again. She was ready to leave. We were depressed. But, whoever comes has to go someday. That's the rule. She handed over another document over which Mr Sitharaman signed. She left the house, taking our hearts as well.

"Do you know how much the bill was?" Mr. Sitharaman wanted all of us to guess.

"Maybe 25" Gowardhan started.

"35" I guessed.

"55" Varma.

"100" Mr Sitharaman.

"What?" We all three screamed in unison.

"100 pounds? Eight thousand rupees for 3 hours?" I couldn't believe it. "That's too much; even engineers couldn't earn that much. 8000?"

"What Gowardhan? Want to start?" Mr Sitharaman tickled.

"But who will hire him when gorgeous options are available." I suspected.

"Even straight girls will hire another girl, but not him." Varma taunted.

"Okay. Let's go out now." Gowardhan reminded me of the time.

"Don't freak out, you know what - you can hire a naked cleaning service," Varma informed in a low voice later that night.

"Naked cleaning services? Means what?"

"Naked girl or boy, whatever your choice is, will come and clean your house."

"Who told you?"

"I know," Varma confirmed. That whole day, he must have researched that.

The next morning, I heard Gowardhan speaking with Mr Sitharaman.

"House is cleaned. Pleasant I feel. Now, no need to look at it at least for a month. After a month, we again can call the service."

"Yes, of course."

"Please, let me know before choosing the service. Please?" Gowardhan requested humbly.

Cloud 10

The elevator door of a skyscraper opened. We were on the penultimate floor of the forty-second story building in central London. That wasn't any less than cloud nine. We felt above cloud nine. There were huge LEDs displaying only the company logo in the reception. That confirmed we were at the right place. We all were in our best possible formal attire on the first day at the office.

"But have you noticed, there is no record-keeping system. No biometric, no RFID, nothing?" Gowardhan's first reaction.

Eva, the office admin, was in charge of introducing us to the whole office. One by one, she started introducing us to the teams. Keeping smiles on our faces, we followed her. Her enthusiasm and interest did not fade anytime, or at least, she did not let us know that even if it was.

Faking a smile is not an easy job. My mouth started to hurt. I appreciate Eva and all like her.

"Do you know what's requisite for her job?" I murmured at Gowardhan in between the smirk-exchange session.

"What? Common sense?"

"Ability to wear the smile for long."

The office was huge, and considering the density of employees, it looked scarce. It was equipped with all the things needed for an office, and also the things that were not needed for the office. There were bean bags which were occupied most of the time, and also there were tall, uncomfortable wooden chairs which were never occupied. The desks of employees were neat and clean and often found with a toy. Westerners worship super-heroes, animated characters, cartoons, and love to have them on their desks. The desks were decorated with table statues. Few of the employees kept their kid's adorable pictures. Others were preserving their vacation pictures. Few desks were seen with Dilbert's cartoon calendar, and some of them safeguarded sarcastic quotes. People's desktop wallpapers were creative, and most of the time funny - with dark humour and office quotes. The individual desks were not looking like individual desks. Gowardhan pointed out - even our doctors don't have such large tables for their patients. Desks were motorized to manage its height. So, if an employee wants to work sitting, it was not a problem, and if they want to work standing, that was easy too. Just on button press it was possible.

"That's out of their necessity. First world problems. Obesity." Gowardhan thought I didn't figure out the moving desks.

"Have you noticed?" Gowardhan asked in amazement as if he heard some south Indian speaking fluent Hindi.

"What?" I looked around expecting some beauty nearby. "What?" I repeated as I couldn't find any.

"Haven't you noticed Varma's accent?" He asked further. I was right; there was no beauty nearby.

"Not really. Why?"

"He has completely changed it. In fact, he is faking it."

"Is it? Let me listen to him."

After some time when we were again called to meet some white folks, we heard Varma speaking. Gowardhan was right; he was faking the accent. I couldn't control my laughter when I heard 'Aahyy' for 'I'; when in India he used to say, 'Aaaaiii' for the same.

I don't understand why some people fake accents. People, typically Indians, are so engrossed in English that they forget it's just a communication medium, just like other languages. And the funny thing is - in front of whom they fake it are not the one who pay any attention to their accent. Not a single person there asked why there was a difference in our accents. I'm sure; they don't even notice.

"That means, he is not faking it properly," Gowardhan commented.

"I think so," I replied in Varma's fake accent.

It became difficult for us to hold our laughter in between serious moments when Varma used to talk. The next stop of laughter used to come when he used to drop his fake accent in a flow and came to his original, Indian, one.

"Hey, but take care, by no means he gets to know that," I asked Gowardhan.

"What?"

"That we know he fakes the accent and is a topic of laughter."

"Yes. We will take utmost care that he won't get to know. Otherwise, who will give us sudden laughter and news to spread when we go to India?" Gowardhan was sensible.

"What happens in London.."

"Go out of London." He completed the sentence.

Arranging and conducting a meeting is a favourite pastime of Brits working in industries. There were huge meeting rooms with all working gadgets in the office. Isn't that a rare sight for an Indian to witness all working gadgets?

For westerners, for any frivolous issues, there are meetings. Their day isn't complete without at least a meeting. There is a meeting for the whereabouts of a project, and that's totally considerable. But there can be a meeting for deciding whether to order doughnuts or cronuts when the project goes live. There can be a meeting for deciding what temperature the office should be kept. There can be a meeting even to decide the next meetings. For our project, it was decided to have a stand-up meeting daily, and a quick stand-up at the end of the day. There were cross-stand-up meetings every month where the project manager of a different project is involved with a different team. There were gross-stand-up meetings where all the projects of a division come together and indulge in a meeting. To the extent we Indians hate meetings in the office, Brits love them.

Indians jump into the act directly, but Brits play around the bush. They first notify about the meeting in an email and turn on the calendar. With this, they ask all others whether any of their meetings are clashing with the timings. If anyone is clashing, the same process is followed from the start. Indians are super cool about this. The manager or the initiator would come and ask - 'Are you free?' And whatever your answer is, he will say - 'Let's have a meeting.' and the meeting is arranged. And if no room is available at the moment, Indians don't see that as an issue. They can have meetings anywhere they want. In Bangalore, my manager and team lead used to share a bike and happened to have a so-called meeting on their route. Thanks to Bangalore traffic, they never went short of time. And that's a win-win-win situation for all three - manager, team-lead and the environment. Manager for a hassle-free ride, team lead for an assured promotion and onsite opportunity and environment for minimal sort of pollution. Indians are smart.

After meetings, there comes a love of Brits in asking for permission. For grabbing a chair beside you, they will ask for permission. If anytime they need a pen from you, they will politely ask you, "Sorry, but can I get your pen for a moment please?"

In technical stuff, they will always announce and ask for your permission even if you are far away from the task. They will ask for permission before restarting the server system, before releasing something or before coming to meet you.

"Who the hell restarted the hub? I was in the middle of something." I remember my lead once came crimped in my previous organisation. Someone made the mischief without informing. The probability of your pen turning invisible when you return to your desk is huge in India. The love of not returning a pen is immense. Indians don't usually ask for permission for trivial reasons. Brits ask and then do. Indians do and then tell if their deed doesn't go wrong.

"You know, British even asked India before coming for the business and then ruled for many decades." Varma cackled.

"That's why I never believe British and their trait of 'asking for permission'. Lesson learnt the hard way." Gowardhan remarked.

***

What worse can happen to you in the foreign workplace other than losing your passport? A celebration of your birthday in the foreign office.

If you think the way we celebrate birthdays in offices, especially in IT in India is embarrassing, you must visit outside and experience the super-embarrassing birthdays. And if you feel awkward as you are forced to sing a song or tell a joke in front of your known colleagues, what would you say to do similar activities in English in front of a few strangers who try hard to appear as your funny friends? I was infelicitous to have my birthday in the UK forcefully celebrated in the London office. The Human Resource Team, popularly known as HRs, in the office takes care of such celebrations. Non-HR people often don't understand the roles and responsibilities of HRs unless they gawk at the festive celebrations in the office. If you are in your own office, your friends know your birthday, your colleagues know your birthday, and hence it's fine for the HR to inform the whole office about your birthday. But what if you are in a different office in a different country where you hardly know anyone, and somehow HRs get to know about your birthday, informs the whole office and few aliens come to wish you?

The Indian birthday celebration system is pretty simple and straightforward. You go to the office on your birthday and HR sends a celebratory copied email. You carry the sweets and in reply to the email, you invite people to have sweets at your desk. People jump on the sweets. People who turn their heads when they see you are the first ones to come and eat most of your sweets. You won't mind and cannot mind as it's your birthday. The team gathers in the pantry in the evening with the cake and snacks if your teammates are young and enthusiastic. You cut the cake and everyone goes back to work after clicking a group picture. This group picture later gets lost in the galaxy. After the cake cutting, you post the mail saying *'thank you for the yummy cake.'* In between, you may be asked to tell a joke or sing a song. You can choose your mother tongue for better effects. If you are a manager, your joke and for that matter any damn activity will have a huge response for obvious reasons. Even if you are not, people may just laugh at anything and keep it to a minimum because they are in a hurry to finish the cake, go to work and then rush home.

But London's birthday was offbeat. Now, it is admirable to receive the wishes online over the messenger because there you are not required to endow a fake smile; but these Brits came to the desk and wished. They first excused themselves, said sorry for taking my time, asked me whether I've some time and then smiled and greeted me. In India, I was greeted with a tight hand-bump on my shoulders. With Brits, it became awkward after I replied with thanks and smiled with an eye contact. What can you expect a stranger to say after that? But these Brits don't mind. They will ask you what the plans are, and how you are going to celebrate. Can they be satisfied if I say I plan to escape from the office before anyone demands a treat and sleep peacefully at home? Isn't this the best way to celebrate? Next embarrassment awaits.

Cake cutting and then eating is not at all a problem, but the birthday song is awkward when you are the centre of attraction. And if you don't know anybody around, it's even more disastrous.

Why do HRs put us through such embarrassments? HRs in the industry are for helping employees and they keep on forgetting this. My experiences with HRs are not great. I get nightmares of them asking for original HRA receipts, reimbursement forms duly signed by team leads, cancellation of comp-offs, informing about the due dates and the work ethics. Ones Gowardhan and I played an HR-rant marathon and decided to come up with the pros of becoming an HR.

"Becoming an HR is not a job, it's the time you are provided for pursuing your hobby. And not just that, you get money too."

"Plus, you get the privilege to interview a few of the people who are smarter than you."

"Plus, you know the salaries of each one of them."

"Plus, you get the bonuses if you cut down their salaries in negotiation."

"Also, you decide the celebration schedule, dress codes and activities."

"Also, you get to interact with guests and rich people and have lunch, dinner with them in expensive hotels on the company's money."

"And and, you don't get fired in recessions."

"And, people need to submit their resumes to you."

"And, you take the final call to hire or not."

"And, nobody messes with you because you are not involved in their work."

"And, your NOC is needed while leaving the company."

We were unstoppable for the whole five minutes.

"But all's not 'well' always for them too. The grass is always greener in the HR department" I stopped the chant as I was out of reasons and shifted the discussion from the HR-rant towards HR-dupe.

"So you want to play the pitfalls of being an HR? In that case, I can't see one." Gowardhan said being unable to spot the yellow hay of the HR department.

"Let me explain it to you very sweetly, this with one example. How do you feel if you are instructed to pack a box of delicious sweets for somebody? I mean, you are allowed to touch and smell, but not eat?"

"How's this even related?"

"Who books a ticket for employees going outside? HR. Have you ever seen HR going abroad like others? They need to watch everyone going abroad and have fun, and what do they do? Book a ticket for them, look out for their accommodation. Just imagine how they must be feeling?"

"Not amused with the example, brother." Gowardhan reviewed.

"But do you know one thing?" I asked, expecting 'no' as an answer.

"I know many things. Which one do you want to know?"

"These HRs are like mothers of the house."

"What? Who? Why is it so?" He questioned, looking at the folk of HRs at a distance.

"Imagine the mother's role and these HR's roles. Their work is intangible. Their efforts go unnoticed. They are hardly recognised for their enthusiasm and hard work. Just think how the company will run without HRs? Exactly like a house without a mother. We don't realise their service unless they disappear. We should start appreciating their attempts to have our life balanced-mothers at home and HRs at work." I realised how HRs helped me with my VISA and all related procedures and thus gave a small tribute as gratitude.

"Yes, HRs as mothers. I need to call my mother. Thanks for reminding me. Sane words." Gowardhan was thinking. After a minute when I prepared to leave, he was still thinking.

"So, by that logic, we all are maids of the house."

"How?"

"Who recruits maids?"

"Mothers."

"Exactly."

*****

Brits mesmerise you with their communication skills. Their mannerism will blow your mind. They know how to please the people around, even strangers, with minimum efforts. Action speaks louder than words, but polite words win the hearts without any action.

"Hello Gentlemen, good morning. How may I assist you?" The security personnel asked us politely on the first day at the office. She issued temporary identity cards and asked us about our country and the journey. She wished us a pleasant atmosphere and a lovely stay in the city. We were not habitual of such politeness, at least not from security personnel. We were impressed with their modesty.

On a phone call, Brits never forgot to ask how we were. Although it must be a part of their telephone etiquettes and they are not genuine about the enquiry, that sounds nice and respectful. It must be appreciated. Surprisingly, Brits get happy when you inquire about them in return. They will thank you for asking them. This way you can easily make their day.

Gowardhan became the victim of such alluring words when he was in discussion with Suzi, a Brit lady, over the phone for work purposes. He started liking her immediately.

"Why do Brit girls sound so nice and pleasant? Why does their voice feel soft as velvet?" He asked us. For him, it was 'love at first voice.'

"You know, they say the couple with different national origins gets nice quality kids." He informed us unsolicitedly. He was thinking about the quality of kids he and Suzi could have.

"Quality kids?" I was surprised at this adjective.

Gowardhan was a firm believer of God and inter-country marriages until he received an automatic reply from Suzi citing her absence from work. The reason was maternity leaves.

We need to remember one thing: our plans and our destiny's plans don't always go hand in hand always. Gowardhan was shattered, broken, and went into the one-day depression mode. That night, he came to us,

"She didn't seem married from her voice and not a mother to be at any cost."

We were unaware about his superpower of identifying the woman's relationship status from her voice.

Indians are simple. Their rules are straightforward. Their etiquettes are elementary. Indians follow only one toilet protocol. Even with ultra high population and limited resources, Indian men don't stand immediately next to others for peeing. There is at least one urinal gap between the two. That's right to privacy in a true sense. Men follow this unofficial protocol sincerely.

Brits are different. There is no concept of a right to privacy, or in fact, no one cares about it. The real shock is when you see no barricades in between the urinals. Even though you don't want to, your eyes take a glance at your neighbour's rocket. Eyes are the crooks. The little monsters want to see everything that mind restricts.

Keeping urinals without barricades is understandable from the employer's point of view. They want their employees to know each other better, personally.

But what about the public urinals? What purpose would it serve to know the strangers intimately?

"Indians hide theirs because we have neither colour nor size." Varma criticised.

"Oh, so if you have both, you must splash to the world?" Gowardhan was disgusted.

"But wait. Who said we don't have size and colour? Is there any guidebook of genitals?" I opposed the whole system of biased rating.

"The great philosophers told the world not to see the outer beauty, but an inner one. I think these Brits did not understand. They took its literal meaning." Gowardhan had the concluding remarks.

But these cultural shocks are not one-sided, they are mutual.
You can take a person out of the culture, but not the culture out of a person.

"My uncle, even after living in Ireland for 20 years, never forgot to have a full glass of tea for dinner." Keralite Mr Sitharaman once bragged after getting nostalgic about his Mallu culture. When in a foreign country, no one can suppress their cultural habits entirely.

After ducks, there comes Indians for having the flexible neck on the earth. Don't ask for the proofs, see it yourselves. Haven't you observed an Indian conveying their decisions without opening their mouth, but swinging a neck in a particular motion?
"But, this ingenious skill of ours is hereditary." said Gowardhan.

"What? How?" I was surprised.

"Okay. See, chewing paan is addictive and is an obsession for us, and has been for many of our ancestors. Till today, *khaike paan banaraswala* makes our legs shake on the dance floor. Paan was life. There is a funny belief among rural women that, the darker the shade of red colour on your tongue after chewing paan, the stronger is the love of your husband on you."

I remember older grannies putting more and more chuna to colour their tongue red to prove their husband's love. Prove to whom? They only knew. Don't know whether that made the colour darker, but that made their tongue burn for sure.

"Necessity is the mother of invention. Here, necessity was to enjoy the paan and not disturb it by opening the mouth to talk. Conveying the message was a necessity too. Then comes the smart Indians to tackle this problem. They invented gestures." Gowardhan continued.

Gestures need not be explained to us, they are self-explanatory. Indians consider these gestures as an unusual part of their life. I don't remember saying explicitly 'yes' with my mouth, and not by my gestures when I was asked to come for tea. Everyone has their set of gestures which the other one understands.

We did not see any trouble in communicating with gestures unless we tried our moves in the UK. In the London office, I was discussing the possibility of diminishing brightness of my new monitor with Harry when Gowardhan shouted,

"Hari," immensely jerking his neck and chin. Harry got confused. Firstly because the pronunciation 'Hari' for 'Harry' got him amazed. And secondly, he did not understand what Gowardhan was trying to say with his neck.

Gowardhan was now not looking at Harry. He was so confident that Harry would get what he wanted to say. Harry thought it was the way of greeting hello. So, he too shouted - "Hello," but Gowardhan was unresponsive. I was an eyewitness and very well knew what they both were thinking. I stopped Harry and said-

"Gowardhan is calling you."

"When?"

"Just now."

"How do you know?"

"He called you; I saw that. Didn't he do-" I jerked my neck exactly like Gowardhan.

"Oh, does that mean - come here? I thought he was greeting me."

We both giggled.

Harry now jerked his chin, moved his eyes, and expressed his desire to excuse him, visit Gowardhan and come back soon.

We giggled again.

Harry was a quick learner no doubt.

"I like it. I like it. Is that the way you communicate?" Harry asked over tea that afternoon.

"Not always, but often."

"That's funny."

"That's innovative, and it serves a purpose." Proud me justifying our gestures.

"That makes sense." Brit came with their usual antiphon.

"That's our daily business. It allows us to be multi-functional. And if you are too keen to witness this more, I advise you to visit any pooja, a religious ceremony, in India. There, understanding gestures are most important. In that ceremony, a pandit, just like a priest, will guide you to perform the ritual only with his gestures because he is uttering the mantras and so can't instruct you verbally. And you need to catch those gestures and perform accordingly. So it's so interesting." I explained the pooja, the strangest way possible.

"Hey" Gowardhan struck in between and signalled me to visit him for a moment.

I signalled him to wait a minute, I would finish with Harry and come immediately after that. Again with gestures. I didn't say anything but Gowardhan understood and left. This whole act left Harry awestruck, again!

***

"There is a big pool table there. Have you seen it?" Gowardhan couldn't control his excitement covered with ecstasy.

"That's snooker, you idiot." Varma pinned his excitement balloon.

"Whatever! Have you guys anytime played it?" Gowardhan turned towards me. By now he has made peace with Varma's base comments.

"I played pool sometimes. Snooker would not be much different. We can play when there's no one around" I stated.

"That would be rare. Let's try our luck." he replied. Again to our surprise, that was not a rare occasion to get a free snooker table to play.

"This is not a fascination for them, I guess. We cry out for such." Gowardhan told me struggling to figure out which end of the stick to hold in hand.

"Yes, just like we don't appreciate the brown skin and they crave for that" I submitted my intelligent reply.

"Fair enough" Gowardhan uttered, holding the wrong end of the stick in hand.

Table tennis is a typical and loved entertainment in the IT industries in India. You can bet on software engineer's TT skills rather than his programming skills. It is also a hint to predict how the company's work culture is. The more skillful the professional in TT, liberal is the work culture or no work at all. If you ask 'So, what do you do in office if you don't have any project?' You'll get 'Nothing man. Just heat up the chair and TT all the day' from a project-deprived software guy. I've seen Chess too in self-proclaimed creative companies and at the most Foosball in startups, but to my pleasant surprise, there was something in the London office I just dreamed of playing for free - Snooker. To be frank, I had never played snooker till that day, but I was smart enough not to reveal it. The smartness lies in what to say and what not to say. The thing I like and adore about Gowardhan is he is not afraid to admit something he doesn't know. That's courageous. I wonder why that can't be contagious. What is better - to be smart or, to be honest?

"Hey, I never played snooker. In fact, I saw it for the first time here and confused it with a pool. Can you teach me a little?" He once requested Harry, his friend by then.

"Yeah man, why not!" Harry reciprocated happily. People are happy to help if you ask them in a genuine way.

Harry, as requested, started tutoring Gowardhan snooker and day by day he started improving and surpassed me. He even started advising me. Life is crazy; a few days back I taught him how to hold a stick and now, he is advising me how to take a topspin. After that Gowardhan was not even asking me to come and play with him thinking I'm easy to defeat and he was levelled up. I too started dropping interest due to my consecutive losses. But I observed one thing - the timing he used to go to play every day. One day, like every other day, I saw him going for snooker but saw Harry working vigorously over his terminal. The doubtful mind did not allow me to work peacefully. I decided to go and see with whom Gowardhan plays. It made me ultra-jealous watching him play with Emma, Scottish tester. Gowardhan did not seem happy to see me there. I as a true friend let them play without the slightest hint of my motive of spying on him.

"Good work chap. You are going forward at F1 pace" I teased him later.

"Harry helped me. I'm helping her. It's as simple as that. Good things you should carry forward." He replied like a mature adult, which he was not.

"But, I know you more than anyone knows you. What's the best scene in the world than a young, beautiful, blonde girl taking a snooker shot?" I continued ribbing him.

"I know what you mean," he said and blushed like never before.

***

The way of looking at a problem and the approach of getting closer to the solution is a very different deal between Indians and Brits. Like, if you go to any British software developer and ask about a problem he might ask you certain primitive questions before going in that direction. He might ask you about something you have never paid attention to.

'What version are you using?' 'Have you unchecked the parity flag and set the debug level to full?' 'What do the logs say?' 'Oh, I think that's a problem related to the network layer. Sorry, but I'm of little help here because I deal with the application layer. Maybe Jose can help.'

On the other hand, Indians directly jump into the problem. For the same problem, they might ask you-

'Was the button Red or Green when you tested?' 'Error message came instantaneously or after some time?' 'Pull off your LAN and try the application, and then reinsert the LAN.' 'Did the same code run yesterday? Pakka?'

So, Indians are solution driven while Westerners are process driven. But if you trace their clues and advice, you ultimately come to the questions which Indians had asked. So, even though the advice of Indians does not look professional, they get you closer to the solution. But not always.

Varma recalled an incident from his previous organization.

"One day when the client's machine did not switch on, they bashed on us. Our team started investigating the same and found out a few files were missing. Somebody had deleted that. Now, there was no way to find who the culprit was. Even it was not clear whether it happened from the client side or our side.

Both- client and we were playing safe and were pushing the ball to one another. Our manager was a hilarious guy. Can you guess what he did?"

"Resigned?" Gowardhan guessed.

"No. In the lunchtime, he fiercely went to everyone in the team and asked in a low voice-

'Sanju, did you remove the files?' 'Barakha, we can recover those files, but mistakenly did you delete those?' 'I told them, Jay. It must be from their side. We have been in this business for quite a long time, and it is impossible for us to make such a mistake. But, what do you think Jay, can it be from our side?' I can't believe how he survived the industry."

***

"Let's ruin the taste buds." I requested Gowardhan one afternoon in the office.

"You mean green-tea?" He confirmed my request quickly.

We headed towards the office pantry to find Harry stirring his tea briskly.

"Taking green tea?" Gowardhan asked to start conversing.

"It's tawny."

"Means?"

"My tea is tawny in colour," Harry responded sarcastically.

"Oh, okay. Let me join you," said Gowardhan. He started making his green-tea beside Harry, who was busy reading the newspaper and dangling the chair. I took my cup and stood at the opposite corner of the table close enough to listen to the interesting encounter about to begin between mordant Harry and guileless Gowardhan.

"I also took the same tea. 'Tulsi Green Tea' and yes, it's brown. Green tea, but brown coloured. Do you know what Tulsi is?" Gowardhan was excited to let Harry know all the health benefits of sacred Tulsi and why he should consume it always. But this time, Harry misunderstood, and he thought Gowardhan was asking him about Tulsi.

"Well, it's grown in the northern part of the UK. It is rich in antioxidants and B12."

"Grown where?" Gowardhan was taken aback at Harry's absurd remarks on India's pride - sacred Tulsi. I signalled Gowardhan to keep calm with a questioning face and let Harry spread out his 'knowledge' about Tulsi.

"Northern UK - like Yorkshire and Lake. And the speciality of Tulsi is, it can only be grown here." We could not believe how anyone can boast so much without a pinch of knowledge.

"Oh, is that so?" I shrieked in between.

Harry excused himself in a minute and went to his desk, leaving two Indians to laugh maniacally. On the same night, Gowardhan repeated the whole incident in front of Varma. We all laughed hard, and suddenly Varma thought of expanding our knowledge base of the UK facts.

"It has always been a habit of Brits to show they know something even if they don't. Like you know, almost two-thirds of Brits lie that they had read the book, even if they didn't appear intelligent and socially aware. And you know which book is their most common lie?"
We nodded in negation as usual.

"My favourite, George Orwell's 1984." Varma revealed.

"Heard for the first time," Gowardhan whispered in my ear.

***

Names depict a lot, not just a name to call. Names help us to imagine the personality traits, albeit they are hardly related. Not only this, we have stereotyped the names as per the job titles. Can you imagine 'Mr Sadashivrao Patil' to be an HR of an MNC firm? It has to be 'Ms Anima Roy'.

In India, names convey one of the most important information - the religion, the caste; and surnames confirm that. Names help us to guess the mother tongue of the people, state they belong to, and so indirectly the states they hate.

'Manjunath' must be from Karnataka, 'Saranya' must be from Tamilnadu, 'Bhavesh' must be from Gujrat, 'Bidya' must be from Bengal and so on. And if they belong to different states, people raise their eyebrows in disbelief. With most interstate marriages, these name patterns are becoming random, hard to guess and eventually to stereotype. But people are too smart. If they find the unusual name, they get into Byomkesh's (an Indian Sherlock) shoes and extract more information.

'Oh, so you are Brijesh Apte. Your father is Maharashtrian; your mother must be Gujarati then. Oh, so the fruit of a love-marriage, uh?'

Westerners suffer from the shortname-usage syndrome. It is logical to use short names for us Indians, because we have long and long names which can make a person hard to breathe if he tries to pronounce the whole name in one breath. Isn't it necessary to use - Venkat for Venkatnarasimha or Mani for Ganeshsubramaniam to save people from short breathlessness?

Westerners have short names, and they make them even shorter and ambiguous, sometimes so vague to not know the gender of the person.

With this idea of using short names in mind, which appeared cool at the first place, we too thought of giving it a shot. Gowardhan took this task on himself and came up with short names for all.

"For you - it's Saand" he calmly disclosed.

"Are you going nuts? You know right what Saand is?"

"Yes, but it suits the way you work, right?"

"Oh, by that logic, yours must be Gobar because it suits what you do here." I bashed a personal attack with a personal attack.

We dismissed this western idea then and there.

"By the way what's Varma's?" I couldn't control my eagerness.

"Feku."

"Why Indian names are so dangerous?" Harry impugned having his biscuit-coloured tea one afternoon in the office.

"Like your surnames?" Gowardhan was immediate.

"What do you mean?" I retaliated immediately towards Harry.

"I mean, look, first of all, you guys have a long and long name and make our tongue go twist and trip in their pronunciation. Isn't it? Why complicate them? You see, names can be short and still serve the purpose. Makes sense? Even our email addresses are shorter than your names."

"See, we Indians always want to kill two birds with one stone and same we achieve with our names. Doesn't make sense to you right?"

"Of course not," Harry chuckled sipping his tea.

"Sorry to say but our names usually have meaning unlike yours. Get me corrected, but, do your names have any meaning?"

"Frankly, I'm not sure." Honest Harry accepted.

"If you see our names, it has some significant meaning in some or the other language. Mostly, our name resembles God. For our culture, people equate chanting with worshipping. You call someone's name, you chant and indirectly worship. Don't you?"

"It's an insane logic dude."

"Insane, but can you deny its sanity?"

"I'm not even on that level. Let's agree upon this, tell me one thing - are all the names belong to some or the other God?" Harry seemed interested.

"Just in Hindu culture, we have 330 million Gods. And I'm pretty sure you don't even know that many words of all the languages you know combined. I also don't know those many words and, of course, those many Gods. So, you say anything, and that word can be related to God somehow you never know."

"That's even more insane. I'm not digging into it. What's yours then Gowardhan?" Harry shifted his line of questions.

"Umm, you see - Gowardhan is a hill in Gokul where Lord Krishna spent his childhood. But more than that Gowardhan means who protects and nourishes cows, the universal mother. And his name signifies an enlightened lamp of knowledge, liberty, wisdom and all such good things." Gowardhan provided the exaggerated meaning of my name as well.

"Oh, that's great." Harry wanted to end the conversation, but Gowardhan was in no such mood.

"Do you know the meaning of your name Harry?" Harry's fear came true.

"Umm, it must be some king or ruler or something somewhere I'm not so sure about." Harry finished his tea and prepared to leave.

"It means-" and Gowardhan started laughing. It confused us both watching his hee-haw unexpectedly. "It means persistently harassing, agitated, troubled." He continued. "That's what Google says." He was showing his mobile, continuing his laughter.

This whole episode of finding what's in the name indeed troubled Harry.

Humorously Yours

If you wonder what British people take pride in something meaningful - it is their humour. Few of them claim that it's British breakfast or British tea, but when I had both, I suspect they are sarcastic when they say that. They claim their humour is unique, subtle, and better than most of the nations which are arguable claims. I am yet to understand how the comparison of humour is done and is there any humour index.

"Wit and sarcasm are the pillars of British humour. You may see them understating, self-deprecating underneath their dark humour. You need to be witty enough to catch those because often they use their humour without any expressions on their faces. Otherwise, you may term them fool which makes you fool," one day Varma revealed this information looking at Gowardhan while stressing the last words.

"He is a moron who has a big inferiority complex about Indians which include himself and is an asslicker to Brits. Just see his behaviour with us and with those whites" Gowardhan told me in a low voice who must have been hurt by the remark of Varma.

"Oh, I see. I don't give a damn to him and advise you to follow the same." I was mature.

One of the proud Brits said to me-

"Sarcasm runs in our blood just like Vodka in Russians."

"Are you sarcastic?" I taunted him within a second. Taken aback he asked me further - "What runs in your blood?"

"Patriotism," I was instantaneous as if I was prepared.

"Fair enough," he said and started drooling over the newspaper he carried.
I won the conversation without any doubt by Indian standards. If someone starts minding their own business after an argument, it is a sign of your victory.

Our manager in London was a core British man. More often than not, his responses made us chuckle. His occasional sassy comments were perfectly timed. Like someday his associate asked him about the whereabouts of the client and when did they send him specifications to which he replied,

"I think it was when Jesus was born."

Or when he is asked what the quarter targets to present before the client, he would say-

"I have a very special something to offer to him. My middle finger."

"Did anyone from the Client side get back to you?"

"Naah! I think he passed away!"

When someone is going on an extended leave, they will warn-

"Call me only if you are dying," and if you ask when they'll return, they will reply-

"Maybe after World War III."

"But where are you going?"

"Jupiter via Pluto."

Walking down the street one afternoon which seemed like noon, we got across a restaurant whose outside board read - 'FREE LUNCH' in a big font with the design. With heavy hunger and hopes, we went near the board which read further - 'FREE LUNCH' and beneath that - 'There is no such thing as a FREE LUNCH'. How cruel!

On the same street, for a service apartment to rent out, an advertisement read - 'No place like HOME' and just beneath it in small letters, it continues - 'and it ain't home. So, get in.'

Gowardhan opinionated one day-

"These British people are not sarcastic. They are rude and just because they are white, their comments are taken in a humorous, sarcastic way even though those are coarse and disrespectful many times."

Brit sarcasm is popular because they have publicised it. But, after living more than 25 years in India, I think Indians are no lesser than anyone, let alone Brits. We've learned sarcastic skills from our parents at an early age.

Indian kids do not get pocket money provided their parents are yet to be influenced by the western practices. Indian kids and teenagers need to ask for money whenever required and provide a precise reason for the demand. They often get less than demanded with more reasons of how the demands are shooting and money doesn't grow on trees. Indian parents always pass sarcastic comments on their regular victims - their children. These skills are hereditary to us.

At an early age, Indian kids are so much exposed to the sarcasm that they sometimes don't understand whether it's for real.

In the office, people call one man - Internet Explorer. After a few days, I got to know people go to him only to ask about other people just like the poor browser used for installing other browsers.

Indians are getting updated with technology, and so is with their techno-wit. I once called a nearby restaurant who started an app-based home-delivery system.

"I placed an order half an hour ago, and still, it isn't delivered," I complained.

He asked for an order number. I provided.

"Another twenty minutes, Bhaiya." He calmly responded.

"Twenty minutes more? Your app says delivery in 30 minutes."

"Then, eat the App!"

"Hey, that's not done. App says the order is ready."

"That is not."

"But, your app-"

"You believe the App or me?"

"App."

"I'm the cook who will cook your order."

We went on a tour from London to its countryside on a sunny Sunday. We were provided with a tall old British man with a heavy British accent and all its indigenous features. On the bus, he asked are there any Australians on the board. When we reached the Stonehenge, it was almost a world wonder which is quite famous for its unique stone structures which are supposedly built some five thousand years ago. The old guide requested all to gather near the visitor centre entrance. He asked -

"Where is my Australian friend?" On seeing him, he further continued - "I want to thank Australians for this, and you all should too. Because Australians built this." On seeing the confused and surprising expressions of all, he knew he had succeeded with his wit. He further continued-

"Nah! Not Stonehenge, but this visitor's gate five years ago. And more thanks for keeping the roof of it hanging." He did not leave the opportunity to taunt the Australian for the hanging rooftop.

Bath is a nearby town from London. It is famous for naturally occurring hot water beds and thus the hot water irrespective of the chilly winter. When the same tour reached that place, old Brit started-

"The water you'll be seeing inside is hot. You need not touch it. Please, believe me. I am an old man, and there is a saying - an old man will die, but won't lie. I know you haven't heard it because I just now invented it. So, you are not allowed to touch it. Not by hand, not by legs, not by any of your organs. And don't ask me whether swimming is allowed. But don't be disappointed dear, due to God's grace and the entry fee we are paying, you'll be allowed to drink hot water as much as you want at the exit. The water is so rejuvenating, believe me, you'll be ten years younger after drinking it."

Perplexed by the taunts thrown at Stonehenge, the Australian tried to pull the leg of the old man. He asked -

"Jon, how old are you? You must be coming here regularly, right?"
Jon, the witty English guide replied,

"Well, don't tell anyone, but this place, I only built around two thousand years ago. I'm a frequent rejuvenating water drinker, you know!"

I was exploring DSLRs in a store in London and wanted to know the prices of various models, so I asked the salesperson whether they have any pamphlet or something to which he asked me -

"Do you have a computer?"

"No. Here? Umm. What?" I fumbled.

So, he asked further in a slow tone - "Do you have a computer anywhere in the world?"

I said - "Yes, I have."

"So, you can go to wherever your computer is. Make sure you have the internet and open our website.

You'll get all the prices required for all the products you want and the products you don't want."

If this is the case in India, the salesperson must have brought some paper from somewhere and would have given all the details in writing. I missed my customer friendly store executives.

***

"Elephant in the room." Manager declared in the stand-up meeting.

Gowardhan turned back to ensure. I pinched him tightly.

"This particular client is a squeaky wheel. He wanted to update the entire codebase, and why, I don't have any idea. I asked him why he was fixing it as it ain't broke yet, but no success. We need to take quick action and put in some integrative work. I won't beat around the bush, what I'm thinking is we'll merge the teams - two heads are better than one, isn't it?" and he continued for another five minutes with other plentiful metaphors and proverbs, half of which we couldn't connect to. But that was pleasant to hear.

English idioms are an integral part of the British language and their dialect. Of course, as it's their mother tongue, they must be proficient and remarkably foolproof of its usage.

"It's the country of greats like Shakespeare and Charles Dickens. We, not in our dreams, can match their English dexterity and perfection. And better, we don't even try for that. At the least, if we can understand what they are saying, that's more than enough." One Sunday evening, Varma summoned us when Gowardhan complained to him about the tough language used in Shakespeare's Hamlet.

"But where did you get the Hamlet?" I asked, ignoring Varma.

"That's on the bookshelf there."

"What other books are there?"

"Everything like that. Tough to get the title and even tougher to get the meaning."

And that's how the bookshelf in our house became no man's land.

"Even Varma didn't get anything about their English, you know? Just on the first day, I saw him inspecting the books, but after that not anytime he delved into the shelf." Gowardhan talked about his observation.

"Yes, maybe. I too feel so. Do you remember he went to watch Shakespeare's play last Sunday night and how he made ho-ho of all that? And he was so silent and lost after watching it. Later, he never mentioned it. I'm damn sure he did not understand anything." I seconded Gowardhan.

"Even if he had told us any hobbling story, we had believed it. Who likes to argue with Varma anyway?"

"He is not witty like his favourite Brits."

"Agree."

English metaphors are on the tongue of Brits. After all, it's a virtue of great writers and poets.

"They use meaningful metaphors; we use meaningless swears." Varma pointed.

"Who told you our swearings are meaningless? They are quite innovative." Gowardhan wanted to play with the fire.

"Va te faire enculer" replied Varma, which he must have practiced a lot, and left the room.

***

What pisses Brits off? Breaking the queue.

'In the last hundreds of years, we never broke it. How come you did, fellow?' They must be thinking to themselves with 'what shit you just did there' expressions if they see someone cutting the line. You will find queues anywhere and everywhere, and also where you least expect it. It titillates them witnessing a queue and being in a queue. If there are thousands of unorganised Brits at one place, the quickest thing they could do is organise a queue. No matter what the situation is, or what place is, the Brits can form a queue, and then breathe a sigh of relief.

"It is illegal to jump the queues at a few places" Varma once added to our knowledge and made us less prone of getting arrested.

"Yes, we know that," I lied.

Having queues is a systematic and sophisticated approach in the first place, and if you see a queue of Brits and how they maintain the distance, that will blow your mind. How Indians maintain queues and how Brits do that are entirely different. Indian queues are jammed like most of the other sites, and people tend to stand close to each other almost touching each other. So, if a first person gets an electric shock, electricity will flow within all. Our queues are hardly straight. Due to space constraints and sharp mathematical skills, we have always shaped them as per the best-optimised space algorithm.

But the UK queues are never other than straight lines, never. Sometimes, you may make a mistake drawing a straight line with a ruler; that would be less straight than the queue Brits form. They don't stand close. They at least maintain a distance of accommodating one more person in between. Those queues are so sparse that you may hardly think that's a queue. And they expect others to adapt to this skill, and elongate their straight queues as we do our patriarchy. But that does not happen every time both with - patriarchy and the queues.

One beautiful day, Gowardhan and I decided to visit the nearby restaurant with a difficult name famous for delicious burgers. As expected, there was a queue. We continued the queue.

"What will happen if a snail comes here?" Gowardhan asked.

"She will reach the counter before us," I replied, looking at the sweeper coming towards us.

"Exactly" Gowardhan shouted, looking into his watch.

We were not too far from our target. When there were hardly 4 to 5 in front of us, the sweeper kindly requested to give her a side to clean. When she was doing her business, we were doing ours - check out the menu card stuck on the top of the counter.

"Just one burger for you. Haha!"

"That's bliss. You chose yours. Get confused."

"What veggies can say more?"

"At least, we know what we are eating. Unlike a few non-vegetarians who think of a chicken, and get pork," I taunted him over last night's dinner.

By the time we were having this discussion, we did not realise when the sweeper had left, and we were out of the queue.

"Hey, you!" Someone shouted.

Baffled, we started looking around.

"Yes, you two!" It was coming from the counter. A white lady with colourful hairs was shouting at us. "Do you think they all are stupids? Come into the queue" She continued, now with a more intense and heavy voice.

We were embarrassed. That was the first time we were shouted at. That was the first time we heard a white lady shouting. That was the first time we thought that was too rude, and that we should pay that back with interest.

"Sorry" we shouted, waving our hands in an apologetic sense as per our Indian habit. We immediately returned into the queue.

"Look now, how I teach that parrot a lesson" I was determined. Varma's sentence 'Nearly 50% of British people cannot do basic maths. Indians are the gem of Mathematics.' was humming in my mind.

"One veggie delight with Fanta please," I ordered softly.

"We don't have Fanta" she replied with rude eye contact.

"Well, what's that then?" I pointed at the lady picking Fanta from the other counter.

"That's F-A-N-T-A." She harshly pronounced. In her eyes, I was a villager from Asia.

"Okay. That's it. Place the order."

"That would be 659" she replied quickly.

"Here it is." I took out a 50-pound note, the greatest thing I had, and placed on the counter.

Her expressions explained she was dazed. She seemed tense because of the complex calculations she'd to do as per their standards. Now, it was her turn to do the math and return the money. She seemed lost and helpless. Usually, people out there pay with a card, so that's rare for the operator to do calculations.

"Okay, " she muttered and started the calculations, but her failure to do so was visible.

First, she took out three 20 pound notes and kept my note in the drawer. Then she put one 20 note in the drawer and brought two 10 notes. Then she put one 10 note again in the drawer. She now had two 20s and one 10 for my 50. She then put two 20s into the drawer and immediately took out for no reason. Her face turned pale. Ours were, with a grin. She kept aside two 20s and concentrated on one 10.

"Should I give you 9 pence more?" I asked her to double her confusion.

"You paid more than required, so I'm going to return to you, Sir."

"Yes, I know. If I give you 9 pence more, that would be 650 and so easy to calculate."

"Okay." She muttered, not understanding my explanation.

"Or in addition to 9 pence, should I give you 50 more pence?" I put another option to push her into a confusion grave.

"Okay"

"Or one more pound?" I said, looking at the other counter which was processing at the double of her speed to make her more flustered. People behind me were getting annoyed by then. Gowardhan who was in supporting role rose his hands and gestured - 'What the hell is going on?'

"One pound and fifty-nine pence make you return 45." I simplified.

"Okay," she muttered, turning red by then.

"Is there a problem?" One concerned Brit genuinely shouted.

"No. She is confused with simple calculations" I replied to him.

"Is that okay? Give me 45 then." I continued looking at her.

"Okay"

"Here it is," I said and put 9-one pence coins and one 50-pence coin.

"Okay. Thank you."

"Or if you want I can give you five pound more," I asked, gulping my laughter.

"Yes, please."

"So, here it is."

"So, here are your 45 pounds."

"No. 50."

"Oh! Yes."

"There." I pointed at the 50-pound note visible in her drawer.

"Have a pleasant burger." She greeted, giving me a receipt with a sheepish smile.

"Not very pleased," I remarked and left.

First time I was happy about the mathematics we are taught in school, and Indian grocery stores where these calculations are effortless.

"Next please." She called out now in lower volume filled with utter embarrassment.

"Same order." Gowardhan expressed with a 50-pound note in hand. "And sorry. I don't have any change."

Her pale face turned paler.

Was Varma authentic with his fact about Brits and Mathematics? Well, I need to have an encounter with another Brit to confirm then.

***

What's the typical hobby of most of the Brits?

Apologising. Apologising for every reason. Apologising for any reason.

The metro train stopped at Paddington, and half of the folks got down, even the old man sitting beside me. A lady was standing. As she noticed a vacant seat beside me, she started her way to the seat. She came nearby.

"Sorry. Can I,"

"Yes."

"Sorry. Can I take the seat there?" She pointed to the seat beside me.

"Sure."

"Thank you so much." She occupied herself and passed on a grateful wide smile towards me as if I had gifted her the seat. We were surprised as to why people were sorry when it was not their fault anyway.

A man in his thirties joined the queue. He smiled and said sorry to me, maybe because he thought I was not expecting anyone behind me in the queue.

I glanced at a smiling infant in a pram and smiled back. His mother smiled at me and said sorry maybe because she thought her infant asked for my attention.

One pleasant evening, Gowardhan and I were walking on the footpath, and a couple was coming from the opposite. As the footpath was not wider, unknowingly out of habit, Gowardhan reached behind me and formed one line. The couple while passing exchanged smiles with copyrighted sorry. The man smiled, said sorry to me. The woman smiled, said sorry to me. The man smiled, said sorry to Gowardhan. The woman smiled, said sorry to Gowardhan.

That was a daily business for us to receive a lot of 'sorry' and 'thank you' for no particular reason. Within a few months in the UK, we received tenfold 'sorry's, and 'thank you's than we did during our lifetime.

"Let's earn as many sorrys as possible, as after a few days, they will be extinct," I instructed others.

Brits don't spare nature too for being sorry. They are sorry for bad weather. On a gloomy, cloudy morning, you may be wished with, "Sorry for the bad weather." As if they are solely responsible for it.

"But you know the Brits are infamous for cribbing about the weather also. You can catch them denouncing the weather all the time." Varma updated.

"Hilariously ironic" I responded, watching a parked bus whose display read - 'Sorry. Not in Service.'

"But they are not apologetic for the exact reason they should be." Gowardhan had another viewpoint.

"What's that?" Amused Varma asked.

"To Indians."

"Why for?"

"Britain owes reparations to all the colonies they once ruled, especially to India. Do you know how India was when they came and what they made India when they left? They owe us apologies, deep apologies for making the lives of Indians miserable." Gowardhan made his point.

"I know whose videos you are streaming now, you are exasperating farrago!" Varma chuckled.

***

People need recognition. Recognition of their good work. Recognition of their intelligence. But Brits are slightly different. They want recognition of their senses as well.

I share with you a secret. I've decoded their pattern about how with minimal usage of the language you can satisfactorily interact with them. Proficient English isn't the primary tool to survive in the UK. Learning the words - Sorry, Excuse me, Thank you, Sure, and Please would suffice. You are half done with these words. Also, we have gestures to communicate. Gestures are universal. And if you not only want to engage in a conversation but also impress them, you need to add one more sentence to your vocabulary. It is - 'That makes sense'.

It gives them the feeling of their common sense, intelligence, and presence of mind.

So, if you tell them - 'I'm feeling damn thirsty,' a concerned Brit will respond with-

'Hey, get some water then.'

And now, you have an opportunity to win the heart and blow their mind. You must say-

'That makes sense.'

The result - Happy Brit!

Imagine you are going to buy a greeting card for your beloved one. You go to the store and store keeper asks you what you want, and you say - 'I want a greeting card for my mother.' And here is the simplest trick to make that storekeeper extremely happy when she asks you to look into the 'FOR MOM' section. You should say - 'Oh, mothers card is in 'FOR MOM' section? Thank you. That makes sense', and I bet you'll get a discount and an opportunity to see a delighted Brit.

Obvious common sense when flattered with 'that makes sense' delights all the senses.

The thumb rule is, to win Brit heart, you should say 'that makes sense' even though it does not. Little appreciation for the obvious thing can make them happy. But that's not always the case in India. If you appreciate someone, that person gets doubtful about your intentions. Or that person may feel you're sarcastic. If you genuinely compliment someone in India saying- 'Thank you. You are really wise,' then based on your tone and expressions, that person may feel you are taunting. You may involve in such conversation-

'No no. I'm mad.'

'No, no, I don't mean that.'

'No, no, so you mean I'm mad.'

In India, you need to be genuine enough so that the person should not feel you're *ingenuine*.

***

People need a change from their routine life. They need entertainment. They need enjoyment. We should be thankful to our Gods for creating so many events in the past resulting in festivals in the present. Festivals are pleasant. They are lively and fun. India is blessed. India is fortunate. Others are not. Whoever doesn't have enough festivals, created days. Days are lame; festivals are for real.

"Days are nonsense." Gowardhan wondered.

"Why so? How are festivals then?" Varma opposed.

"Think. What's the purpose of Mother's Day or Father's Day? Do you think it has to be so formal to celebrate days to express your love towards your parents?"

"But, but, maybe it is as kids are not so close to their parents. Kids often leave home sooner they find their partner or a job, whichever is earlier. These days are the remembrance for them. They need an occasion to express their compassion towards their parents. They have to be formal." I oiled the fire.

"Point." Gowardhan joined me.

"You guys have some serious misconception." Varma excused.

The UK is no exception to the day culture. We witnessed Valentines week in London. The streets were red with greetings, gifts and flowers. On enquiring, it was evident that flowers were too expensive.

"Floriculturists must be millionaires here. How can we export flowers from India to here? Do you have any idea? The IT industry is boring. We need to look for the second income source. So, you know or not?" Impatient Gowardhan wanted to shift from IT to flower business looking at the prices of the flowers and bouquets. Curious, he went ahead and held a bouquet in hand, "No way! The love is too expensive here. Look at the price of this bouquet?"

Converting it turned out a bouquet was costing more than a thousand rupees.

"No way, it is way more costly. In India, with that money, you can book a lodge for a few hours and have some more love." I knew Indian psychology.

But, the cost didn't affect Brits from buying expensive flowers and gifts. The red shops were huddled with lovers which were deserted other days.

"Just look at there" Varma pointed to the Mother-Daughter pair. "Do you think it is possible in India for mother-daughter to go Valentine shopping together?"

"I'm not saying anything. I've very dirty thoughts in mind." Honest Gowardhan smirked.

"Like always." Varma wasn't impressed. "In one way, we say kids don't have much attachment with their parents, and when we see them together, we can't digest. Isn't it ironic?" He further said.

"Makes sense." I supported his logical statement.

"What makes sense? What I just said? Or your stereotypical thoughts?"

"Your statement."

I was expecting a smile.

"Don't use their patented words. Doesn't suit you." He slammed instead.

A few people don't even understand who is on their side and who is not.

Next showed up mother's day. Everyone got sentimental with their mommies. Shops, malls got decorated with posters and advertisements with mid-aged models crafted as mommies. Gowardhan too couldn't control his emotions and fell prey to one of such advertisements. His emotions won against his pocket, and he bought expensive Armani perfume for his mother.

"Are you not buying anything for your mother? Any gift?" He asked me.

"I'll give her the greatest gift any Indian mother wishes for." Cold-blooded me replied.

"What's that? Hard cash?"

"Authority to choose a wife for me."

You, the folks

India is a young country; others are not that fortunate. The average age of the UK population is around 40 years. That implies there are a lot of older people, and you realise that when you look around while roaming. You see old people everywhere - on the roads, in gardens, on the hills, in cinema halls, in malls and, of course, in hospitals. But their activities make you amazed. And if you compare their operations with that of Indian old folk's, you'll be stunned. Except at the hospitals, they are so different.

Where do you see most of the old people in India? Homes, temples, garden benches, isn't it? Even though their virtual presence is everywhere, especially in their children's lives, they restrict their physical presence mostly to their homes. But the UK's case is distinct. I've seen these oldies jogging, trekking, playing football. Even once we witnessed an old couple kissing ruthlessly on a subway.

"That must be an extra-marital affair." Gowardhan judged. I ignored him. I ignored the old couple too, but Gowardhan was looking as if he was enjoying himself. Maybe he was. I pulled him when he was shouting "Look where his hand is. Look where his hand is-" and we went our way.

One evening, I was jogging with Gowardhan by my side when one granny surpassed us. She was in her jogging suit with wireless headphones on. It gave us complex, not only because we were in our jeans and she was in befitting attire, but the granny surpassed us. Granny?

"My shoes are not running shoes. They are old just like the granny. They lost grip and reduced my speed. Yours are perfect. You should run faster."

I overlooked Gowardhan's excuse and continued looking at her.

"Have you ever spotted such granny in India?" I asked him.

"Our grannies are different. They don't want to roam, leave aside jogging. And you know what I find funnier? They don't let their children and grandchildren either. My grandmother, she always restricts me from going out in the evening. 'It's dark outside. Don't go' she used to order. 'Sit at home. Watch some TV. Read something. See, there is a newspaper. We all are here. Talk with us. Come here. Sit. Why go outside? What's there so special outside? Why do you want us to worry all the time? Don't you want us to have a peaceful life? Chant God's name for good. Come here. Sit.' She says all the time." He continued.

"You know what the ultimate aim of my grandma is? Get me bathed early in the morning. No matter what day it is-holiday or working day, Sunday or Monday, whether I'm sick or tired, she wants me to get bathed early. 'Go, get bathed, what are you doing? Sleep after the bath. Bath, and you'll feel fresh. Go. Bath and then get the breakfast, don't do the reverse. Go bath.' When I'm in my sleep, she comes and asks- 'Have you bathed? Go bath first, and then wake up'. I mean just stop it." I expressed my Grandma's concern.

"You know what my grandma's favourite word is?" I continued.

"No?"

"Yes, that's right."

"What?"

"No."

"No, what?"

"No is the word. Her favourite word. No. No all the time. Whatever I ask her, she replies with NO. Can I go, and before I complete the question, her response is ready - No. In summer she says - No, you can't go because it's very hot outside. In the rain, she says - it's raining outside and the winter - it's very cold outside. I don't know what to say."

"Mine is also similar. She counters me with - why. Why do you want to go? Why at this time, why not tomorrow morning? Why so late? And here. Grannies must be saying to their grandchildren - 'Hey, why are you home all the time? Let's go jogging. What're your weekend's plans? What about hiking this weekend? Or I'm running a marathon this Sunday. Jon, do you want to join?" I said affirming him.

"But wait. Do grandparents live with their grandchildren here?"

"That's the difference." Varma made the implicit guest appearance into the conversation. "Steve went for a holiday in the US with his mom and grandparents. They all had sky-diving there. Even his grandparents." Varma, the un-appointed lawyer of Steve, notified.

"If my grandma knew people do such things on their foreign visit, she must have stuffed something in my mother's mind to cancel my onsite plans." Gowardhan recited.

"I wish she did," Varma mumbled loud enough for me to hear but Gowardhan.

"Let's think about this. In India, all our elders bar us from adventures. Don't do that, don't go there, and all that shit. But see the difference. Here, elders not only encourage but they too participate and enjoy. Indians are shit scared!" he continued.

"Maybe. But, that's also a part of the cultural differences and upbringing." Gowardhan muttered.

"What man! This is not relative; this is absolute. Absolute difference. We dump whatsoever in the name of culture." Varma roared with his mathematical clarity.

"In that case, I'll tell you a unique, adventurous thing about Indians." Gowardhan looked confident.

"Shoot"

"The thing only Indians do and Brits can't even imagine."

"Yes, go on."

"Let's think about this. Even with joint families or with nuclear houses with no facilities of separate rooms, Indians do sex, a lot of sex, and reproduce. See our numbers. Isn't it an adventure - having sex when your parents are in the house? Or your children in the same room? How adventurous! Also, Indians adventurously moan in their mind because they are not allowed to make any sound. Living with several people, and still keeping alive romance is an adventure. Indian sex life is adventurous, and nothing can beat that."

"Wow! So adventurous." Varma resigned and left the place immediately.

***

The legacy of sophisticated behaviour is inborn in Brits. The mannerly kid is a myth I thought. But to my surprise, the kids were well-behaved and never looked crying or demanding. On the other hand, our Indian kids are embarrassing ninjas. It is not surprising for a kid to put parents in utter embarrassment in an unimaginable way. I'm sure every parent in India must have gone through this horror. It is people's common hobby to ask a child who is their favourite - mom or dad in front of both. But, how embarrassing it would be if a child says- None?

Brit kids are so sophisticated that if you ask the same question to them, they may say - 'I'm extremely sorry mom, but right now my inclination is towards Dad. I'm apologetic if you are hurt in any way. Love you, mom. Sorry.'

Indian kids behave differently in social circles. The parents are enthusiastic to show their talkative child's traits in gatherings, but many times that ends in awkward situations.

"Show uncle, where is the doggy? Do you see doggy nearby?" A mother expects her toddler to show everyone a dog sitting aside, but instead, the child turns towards his Dad.

It is a routine practice for a Brit couple to go on outings with their kids. You often see around the whole family enjoying a place. Even, there are family discounts on entry tickets.

"I do wonder sometimes," Gowardhan said, scratching his head, looking at the entry ticket board at London zoo.

"About what?" I asked.

"Look. There are family discounts. For two children, for three children. Do you think Brit couple has 2-3 children?"

"There has to. Not every couple, but some. Otherwise, why would there be discounts?"

"Maybe." He said, not fully convinced looking at a couple with four children.

"Look there. 4 children." He pointed to the family of six.

"Yeah. See, just now you were wondering. But they look so young to be the parents of four, don't they?"

"Yes, they do. But we don't know whether they are their children. I mean-two maybe their own children, one may be the only husband's from his previous wife, and one may be the only wife's from her previous husband." Gowardhan passed a mischievous smile.

"I don't know what your problem is." Varma dashed into the conversation.

Gowardhan must've gulped the word 'you'.

***

London is a city of pets. You can often witness a well-behaved pet with a couple. I'm saying well-behaved just because I haven't seen a dog barking on any pedestrian or a car or even on their rivals- cats and dogs of other areas. These pets are half human. They will give you side while walking. They mumble-sorry, thank you, and excuse me while crossing. They are humble. They mind their business. Dogs are calm, composed, and well-educated about sex-awareness. It is impossible for you to spot the dogs clamped together back to back as a result of sex went wrong. They dress up appropriately as per the occasion. This scenario is entirely different than what you find in India. Clamped dogs from the back is a common sight. Fights between pet dogs and stray dogs are frequent. In the UK, you find neither. Neither stray dogs nor dogfights.

Having a pet has a different meaning in both cultures. Indian pets, especially dogs, are for security purposes, and thus their training goes in that direction. While in the UK, I don't think dogs serve this purpose. Those dogs don't know how to bark which is the primary requirement of a security guard. UK pets are like companions; they are treated and trained in that direction. I asked one local about this, and he explained.

"Frankly, you see, the marriages are not that stable here compared to India. It is an open secret that we need a companion until our last breath. We feel insecure; we feel lonely like everyone else. Pets are the best options we have. We love them to the core, and they love us back. We want them to be with us all the time. After all, no man is an island."

In India, it is difficult to distinguish whether the dog is a stray one or someone's pet. My friend had a pet dog. During the day, he used to force the dog to go out of the house and find food for himself. We give lessons to our pets for becoming independent, but not to our children at the right age. And that smart guy used to call this pet at night to secure his house. A dog used to affirm and never complained. Pets are innocent; humans are not.

Two Australian interns during my IIT days used to ask me every time they sight a street dog, "Whose dog is this one?" What could I say? I used to say - "They are God's dogs. Haven't you sometimes sighted dogs in the temple?" They used to get surprised, nod in disbelief but didn't ask me about this further. They knew - you don't mess with Gods in India. God is a universal sink for us. We can dump anything in God's name.

Morning sunlight gets adored by Brits. They always spare time and go for a stroll where they can catch plenty of natural sunlight and make their bones strong. Indians have over strong bones due over sunlight available. Brits don't forget to take their pets and spouse with them. On such days, the gardens look like a sophisticated pet market but no pet to trade.

We too went for a walk in a nearby garden on such a day primarily to enjoy the atmosphere. The garden was surrounded by joyful people cycling, playing with their pet, children throwing discs, and dogs bringing out to them, a few sunbathing calmly and a few elderly remembering their younger days sitting on the benches. What took our attention was how the pets were behaving. Dogs were sternly following the unsaid instructions of their master without eye-contacting or stalking other dogs. Their mind and body were in sync with the human master. That was astonishing. When you see two dogs in close vicinity, what do you expect? If they are of the same gender-they will bark at each other, and opposite gender tries to have sex, right? We were also thinking the same, but that did not happen anytime.

"That must be because these pets are dressed. Who knows, they might get confused about the gender of another. Our dogs don't dress, so anyone can guess the gender. But here, they hide. Dogs hide, people show." Said Gowardhan and laughed uncontrollably.

"But look at the sophistication of theirs," I replied, watching Labrador hand shaking his master.

"Yes, too much sophistication for dogs. I think there must be condoms for dogs. Dogs must get permission from master and master rewarding him with a condom. How could the shape of the condom be, mate?" Gowardhan asked in jest.

"By the way, if you are talking about the sex life of dogs here, let me tell you one more thing. One more restriction on the UK dogs is they can't have sex with a dog of a royal house without permission. Strange but true." Varma informed.

"Are you sure? What nonsense is this one! And even if that happens, who will be guilty in such a case? That dog? Or his master?" I shrugged out my genuine doubt.

"How miserable sex life of that royal dog is! Must be sex-deprived throughout the life" Gowardhan was inconsolable.

If you compare the lifestyle Indian dogs and UK dogs, I think - Indian dogs must be enjoying much freedom in India. Indian dogs have a choice, a lot of them - to sit on the road, or sit under the tree, to bark or not to bark, to bark on the two-wheeler or to bark on the four-wheeler. They are even allowed to have unprotected sex on the streets. They are not found guilty in many accident cases even though eyewitnesses scream so. India is liberal as far as pet's choices are concerned.

Dogs in India are dudes sometimes. They have their swag at night, and humans better not to mess with them. Certain areas in a city are often claimed dangerous at night due to these dogs and their horror. But no dog is rebelling from birth; the life experiences make them that way. We all make them that way. One night, I was travelling by cab in India and on a lonely road driver sighted a group of street dogs discussing something peacefully. He suddenly increased the speed and honked in their direction, and within a second, the discussion ended, and dogs ran for their lives with frightened faces. I was taken aback. I asked firmly-

"Why are you doing this?"

"It's fun." He told, being as calm as the idol on his dashboard.

I imagine what will happen if these Indian dogs meet their UK counterparts. They will say to each other- 'You ruined our name!'

The case of cats is no different. They are well behaved too. Cats don't have as many privileges as their rivals - the dogs have. These cats are like those Indian village homemakers with limited privileges, whereas the dogs enjoyed the liberty of metropolitans. Cats were hardly spotted in gardens relishing the warm sunshine.

On a cloudy morning, I was waiting for a signal to turn green for pedestrians. One lady beautifully dressed in a fur coat was by my side. An adorable kitten accompanied her.

"I tell you - she must be an animal activist, but must be using animal products like that fur coat of hers." Gowardhan bombarded unsolicited opinions out of habit. The signal turned green. Lady moved on. We moved on. But the kitten was still busy in analysing the signal. Poor kitten got confused, unable to spot her mistress. Her mistress crossed the road and signalled the kitten to come over. Little kitten softly synchronised her paws and gently crossed the street.

"Oh, the black cat crossed so many people. Now they will go ten feet back and then start their journey with God's name" I chuckled at Gowardhan.

"Yes, I bet. They will. After all, it was a black cat. Who will take the risk?" He responded quickly.

Although dogs and cats cover the major portion, there are a lot of others Brits keep as a pet. Varma had a detailed study about this section too.

"British people term fish in the tank as pets too. And, people hire other people to babysit their pets. Gowardhan, you too can earn extra by babysitting fishes in a tank."

The content face of Gowardhan turned vengeful.

"You can find rabbits, hamsters or even pigs and lizards as their pets." Varma was pouring out his study.

"Lizards? Our lizards are unloved all the time." Gowardhan replied with his Indian observation.

"And also if you pet a pig and keep that pig's house, pigsty, in front of your own house, it is a punishable offense. That's one of the strange laws in the world" Varma vomited his knowledge. "You know, Harry has twin mice - Brian and Bruno and Katy have Geru, a tortoise." He continued. We nodded without reacting.

The most inevitable and inescapable question you have to face after you return is - 'Have you got any chick?' No matter how old you are, what your relationship status is or what your personality says, you have to face these types of questions from your kooky friends. You join the new office, you'll be asked. You travel a long train journey, you'll be asked. You shift to the new apartment, you'll be asked. You return from the flour mill, you'll be asked.

There are two mutually exclusive sets of people as far as you are buzzed about girls - your parents and others. Your parents, they will ask you every detail of the foreign country except girls. They are keenly interested in everything and inquire about the weather, work, food, temples, furniture in the house, any snakes on the road, how foreign babies look and every other damn thing but girls. There are no records of them asking about girls. Every pair of parents has their perfect notion about foreign girls, especially whites, and they are not ready to come out of that notion.

'They are witches. They take our sons and do honky-ponky and throw them out. They turn psychos when they see our sons.' This is what Gowardhan's grandma told his mother. His mother advised Gowardhan - 'Be extremely careful', but she didn't tell him from 'whom to be careful'. Moms, you know! They advise, but that's imprecise and the real message is always hidden.

'Take care of yourself and don't go out much, especially at night.' What they mean is - don't go to the red-light area.

'People can bluff you, and it's dangerous.' What they mean is - Don't visit strippers. 'Have fun'. What they mean is talk to them daily, have dinner and sleep.

Their advice is a perfect example of being intentionally non-specific.

The other set of people includes all except parents. This set is more interested than you in knowing overseas girls. These people are excited whether you got laid or how close you were to be. I am unable to recall the number of people asking me after my return - 'How was the strip club?'. Whenever I interacted with my Indian friends while in London, no one forgot to ask - 'How are the white girls? Did you get lucky anytime?' People have this tremendously wrong perception about the western world - that brown people are in high demand. Well, this is sufficiently true, but not to the extent to which we all think it is. These people think white girls are just waiting impatiently to see a brown Indian man. And when they spot one, they go crazy, mad, lunatic, and instantly wink, ask for a coffee and take the brown Indian home.

"I know you went to the strip club. Don't tell me you didn't. No one return from London without visiting those clubs." My Mumbai settled friend interrogated.

"You know what, in India the same thing people from villages say about Mumbai." I just noticed the change in his subject. Why did he change the subject? Because I told him the fact.

We believe racism is prominent, as well as brown people are adored for their skin tone which is contradictory. It is ironic, but notably, both scenarios are for real. It is your destiny that decides what is there for you. You may be admired for your skin tone or may be ridiculed for the same. Or more possibly none can happen. Same with girls. You may get some girl or you may not. But people are not ready to listen to this; they want some spicy stories. They want to hear how you got to the strip club, how the white chick stripped and how you took a lap-dance and had some mushy-mushy naughty time with her. And if you say anything other than this, they will not believe and show utter disappointment, but surprisingly they ask the same question days later in the hope that answer will be changed.

"For God's sake, tell me how the strip club was?" One friend shouted at me.

"I repeat - I didn't go anytime," I shouted further. He then calmly shoved the deadliest weapon.

"Take a vow of your mother and say that again."

UK girls are amazing. Every Indian must admit that even though they haven't seen any.

"That may be because we are bombarded with the belief that white is beautiful, and that way our psychology is trained. No matter what, our brain is biased towards fair colour, and that's not fair." Gowardhan's logic was unflawed like those girls.

"Maybe. Whatever." I didn't want to engage in conversation with him and miss the view.

"But, those girls are amazingly hot."
Only on this element all - Gowardhan, Varma and I had the same opinion.

UK girls are fashionable. They are trendy. They keep themselves neat, tidy, and upright. We never found an ill-dressed girl. They always dress well, put on makeup, and go out with their expensive gadgets. Aside from two houses, there lived a lady who used to accompany her daughter daily till the end of the lane. Her timing was matched with ours. She used to walk only 100 m, but still, she was always nicely decked-up. They don't compromise on dressing and looking well ordered.

"But I don't understand why they put makeup on? They are fair as milk and why on earth do they need makeup?" Gowardhan is girlfriend-less and thus ignorant.

"Makeup is not only to look fair. Maybe they put it to hide pimples we never know." Married and experienced Mr Sitharaman spoke for the first time over the UK girls.

"But I never observed pimples too on their faces."

"That means, they aptly apply their makeup."

"I don't know whether it's in their genes or they regularly exercise or that's God's gift, but look at their figure. Aren't they perfect? Fabulous. Wonderful." Gowardhan was excited when he saw a magical beauty riding her dog across the street.

"That's because you only lure girls who are in perfect shape. You don't look out of shape girls. You can't generalise. There are girls of all types. You don't notice the girls you don't want to notice." Varma said.

"Whatever. Maybe"

The outfits we declare modern in India are quite usual in the UK. The costumes we report 'asking for it' type in India are quite typical there. Intrinsically, hardly anyone gives a damn about what others are wearing in public places. There is nothing unusual to see a mother-daughter pair both in a pair of shorts roaming happily together with a naked dog.

If you want to know what 'skin-tight-outfit' means, you should go and visit some developed western country and witness it yourself. Also, skin coloured skin-tight clothing is commonplace, and that's the highest level of illusion I had ever witnessed.

"Look look look look" Gowardhan tapped my shoulders like a tuning fork.

"Oh my-"

"Oh, oh, oh, I thought she was wearing nothing." He lowered his tapping frequency as our excitements lowered.

"Do they know that outfit can make someone's heart race flying and finally fail?" I was still in awe.

"It did almost ours. But, look at her. I mean, I've never seen such deep skin tight. Even the slightest of the bump and pit on the skin was making an impression." He was accurate. The outfit was so tight that if she had farted, you could see the bulge.

After an hour or so, he again returned to the topic of interest.

"I can't believe it. That's too much. That was too tight. They must have to spend a good time removing those. Don't know whether their skin gets peeled off in the process. And have you seen the impressions? If they had naughty time the previous night and if their boyfriend bites somewhere, that too can be visible on the impression."

"Maybe. Whatever." I cut him short. After all, there was no point in the discussion when there was no possibility of getting to know that from any girl or become their boyfriend and experience it ourselves.

"But, have you noticed?" He was not leaving the subject.

"What?"

"Their physique?"

"That's good."

"No, that's huge. They look heavier than us. Forget Indian girls, even if you and I go and stand beside them, we'll look like Chacha Choudhary."

"Yes, that must be their genes."

"So, they should not be called chicks in slang. Chicks are small."

"Then what should they be called?"

"Chicken."

Another hour later he detected an eye-catching outfit again.

"Oh man. Look at her. How short her hot pants are. They are too short. Isn't it?"

He was accurate in his observations.

"Hey, how would you look in those hot pants?" I put him on a hypothetical question.

"My underwear is longer than that. So, if I wear that, my underwear would be visible."

***

Modernism and PDAs go hand in hand in this era. The countries with higher PDAs are termed modern inadvertently. The UK is the epitome of both. When we think of Western developed countries is a white couple involved in the PDA. PDAs are not uncommon. So don't get too excited when you detect fervorous slobbery lovemaking at any public place.

"London is hugely romantic," Varma said scanning a couple passionately kissing near the Tower Bridge.

"Just because we see people involved in lovemaking doesn't make the city romantic," Gowardhan commented.

"Then, what does? Are Indians romantic?" Varma asked, to which Gowardhan changed the subject.

You will always see couples romancing around you - holding hands, hugging, smooching. Such scenes make you excited and jealous at the same time if you are a mere observer and not the participant. In one glance, you can conclude who is a couple and who is not by their display of affection. In India, it is totally a different case. Here, if you are a couple, you are not supposed to hold hands together in public places, leave alone hugging and smooching. We have separate public places for such activities - gardens, big trees, zoos, autos, fields, and jungles. Funnily, it is perfectly fine and unobjectionable to hold hands or pinky fingers if you are of same-sex adults, but homosexuality is distasteful and often objectionable.

Hugs are common in both countries. In London, you see only couples hugging each other, and in India you see only non-couples hugging each other. The display of affection between 'just friends' is different. In London as a third person, you cannot even slightly guess whether they are friends because they don't show any affection. But in India, you will get confused seeing their affection on whether they are friends or homosexuals. The friendly talks in India could not complete without loud laughs, clapping and occasional hugging. The frequency of these activities depends on the level of friendship. One great thing is we consider everyone as a friend even though we know them bare minimum. We are friends first and colleagues later, friends first neighbours later, friends first strangers later.

In my college days, I interacted with two Australian students who came for an internship. We Indians have this habit of directly targeting the person with personal questions. So, to break the bubble, I asked a casual question - "So, you guys are the best friends?" And was expecting a usual answer. To my surprise, one of the boys said - "We are not friends. We just met by accident, because of this joint internship." And the other was not at all looking at him; his facial expressions revealed he was expecting this, and he would have given the same remark for that. I remember we used to be possessive about our friends. Friends become angry if their friend becomes someone else's best friend. If similar questions were asked to an Indian guy, he would have answered - "Best friend? He is my brother!" Indians are friendly, they want to be friends, and they want to make friends with whoever they meet. Remember Life of Pi?

"Only because Indians don't show affection publicly doesn't make them less romantic." Gowardhan made an out of line comeback to Varma's question about romance.

"Whatever. But if you are good at something, why not show it?"

"If you know you are good at something, why take a certificate of that from others?" Gowardhan was dominating. "If we had not been romantic, we would not be the second most populous." He slammed.

"That's romance without protection, you understand? And without any thoughts, of course." Varma bounced with his final punch.

Thoughts for food

"Long, long ago, our ancestors, the Neanderthals, discovered that raw meat when cooked, boiled or roasted, tastes tasty and the practice of cooking started from there," Gowardhan informed while we were in a queue in London's International Food Court.

"Okay. But why now?"

"No. I think a part of society did not evolve. They still eat raw meat, just look at them-" Gowardhan pointed to a counter where all raw slices of meat were neatly arranged. Those slices were going in between the bread happily as it is - unprocessed, raw.

"How can anyone eat raw meat?" I was a little surprised with this rawness.

"Why not! Just look at that blue-eyed gorgeous." A girl was munching her burger peacefully.

We too were asked on a couple of occasions about our choices subsequently.

"How do you want to have this, Sir? Unbaked, half-baked, or fully-baked?"

"Fully baked please." We always wanted yet another option of double-fully-baked but did find nowhere. Often, we wondered why their fully baked seems like a half baked by Indian standards?

Food is the mirror of the culture.

"Why do you use such terms like 'food.' Use the term 'cuisine.' That's more refined. If you say food, they'll term you gypsy." Varma once slammed me for my ignorance of particulars.

So, the cuisine is the see-through glass of the culture. The cuisine also reflects the status of the country. What grows in the country, what is abundant in the country, and what is rare there as well. If you take Indian, for example, our food is spicy, and so we are rich in spices. We supply spices all over the world and make the world *spiceful*. We have infinite rice dishes; we grow rice. Rice is where happiness lies. We have sweets; we have junk food, we have everything you want. Now, what do we lack then?

If you taste British food, you'll wonder what they have. They don't have much. They don't prepare rice much. What they have is meat. The meat of everything. Lamb, pork, beef, chicken, fish. You name it, and they eat it. And yes, bakery products. The Indian bakery scenario is uncomplicated. We have bread and sweet bread majorly. But, the Brits have a variety of bread; if they change something slightly, they term that as a different dish. So, you have bread. You mix some sugar, you have sweet bread. You roast more, you have roast bread and sweet roasted bread. You don't add sugar; you have non-sugar bread. You can play with numerous ingredients and make infinite permutations and combinations, and make a lot of dishes out of it.

"If you come to Britain, and if you don't have English Breakfast, you must jump into the Thames." Once a colleague advised us.

"Oh, is bathing in the Thames allowed in London?" Gowardhan asked sarcastically.

"Who allows bathing in the river dude?" The colleague was taken aback.

"We do."

If you ask anyone how English Breakfast is, more than the quality, they'll first mention the quantity- it is huge. It is too big to term it a mere breakfast. Like many of the mandatory things, taking an English Breakfast was one of them. The day was decided- one fine Sunday it was. Saturday night, we had a light dinner, so, the next day was the perfect one.

If you want to troll yourself, the best you can do while in Britain is ordering English Breakfast, a vegetarian one. And that's what I did. Gowardhan and Varma opted for the real one.

"Sure." One Brunette smiled after taking my order. She seemed perplexed. I guess they were preparing the vegetarian one for the first time. She must have announced going inside - 'Look, there is an order for Vegetarian English Breakfast. Does anyone know what to include in it and what to remove? Has anyone done this before?'

Exactly ten minutes later, the orders arrived. Before mine, I looked at other plates. They were decorated with a lot of things. I knew who the better person to know all of the items were. Varma introduced me to the non-veg world. Their plates were filled with sausages, black pudding, bacon, and many others. What he introduced as black pudding seemed delicious like a chocolate cake.

"What's that made up of?"

"It's grilled and boiled in its skin with the blood and-" Varma started detailing.

Disgusted, I stopped him midway and looked into my plate. Instead of pudding, I had mushrooms. Instead of sausages, I had several beans and mashed potatoes.

"Coming to the UK and having a Veg Breakfast is like watching a 3D movie without glasses. You'll not get the effect, and you think the film is boring. You are a big fool to order Veg here, and stupid to expect it to be great." I was slammed hard.

"Well, okay. Unfair enough." I accepted and concentrated on boiled mushrooms.

***

Due to excellent command over the language, Brits give the best possible description of the food items making it impossible for you to resist. The alluring and glamorous descriptive words seduce you, make you tempted to try it out, at least once. Won't you fall for the description - crust dumpling with a mellow filling, podded peas soaked until gelatinous, quaggy beans served with comer coriander? Or can you wildly guess what - crack half open, mildly-fried crisp yet brittle piece filled with a fine mixture of potatoes, chickpeas, and onion served with saucy tamarind solvent, could be? Isn't it beyond your imagination if I tell you that was the description of *paani-puri*?

Surviving as a vegetarian itself is a challenge if you are not in India. India is Veggie's Paradise assuredly. And more trouble if you don't understand the fancy dish description people use to fool you. After a long walkover in the National War Museum, I ordered *xxxx*-Potato-*yyyy* imagining it to be a baked potato filled with *xxxx* and spiced up with *yyyy*. The caterer asked me about the options - with creamy butter or with newfangled cheese-butter. To save a few pounds and in turn more rupees, I went with a creamy butter option.

After the description of the item, Brits give utmost attention to packaging. The packaging is glorious just like the description. In the packet, there are more tissues than you use in the toilet. There are more forks than the items inside.

For my potato dish, packaging was as usual attractive. Gowardhan, on the other hand, was enjoying his chicken curry and was giving me and my food box a slanted look. The potato dish had injected excitement in me. The packaging was playing its supportive role precisely. With great precision, I opened the box so as not to let whatever was inside touch the box interior and ruin the show. My hands were shivering due to the excitement, chilly weather, and anxiety of whether this would be worthy of four hundred rupees.

As soon as I opened and had a first glance, I couldn't believe my eyes. How could that be possible? There was just a boiled potato that too not skinned. And what about the creamy butter? There was a small pouch parked itself at the corner of the box. 'Butter' was written over it. I missed India and its delicious items. In India I was fooled, I accept, but not up to this level. It might not have been so embarrassing if

Gowardhan did not see what had happened to me, and voluntarily telling each and everyone that I was fooled for four hundred rupees just for a boiled potato - an unskinned four hundred rupees pesky potato.

***

It was tiring and annoying to look for a restaurant with consumable veg options. I remember going to a particular eatery for straight five days for a veg burger. It used to become mundane after the second day, but there was no other choice. More disturbing was the fact that Gowardhan's non-veg burger was always cheaper than mine.

I love pizza. Everyone does. We went to a store for pizza one day. The store was famous, but one thing they goofed up- they kept everything transparent. We could easily observe how they were making the pizzas.

"They are with gloves. That's nice." Gowardhan said.

"Yes, that's hygienic. But wait."

Pause.

"Did she just insert her hand in the non-veg tin and without changing the gloves mixed them with veg tin?"

Pause.

"Yes, she did the same as you stated," Gowardhan confirmed.

And folks, that was the last pizza I had in the UK.

I couldn't jump onto the non-veg seeking an excuse of unavailability of veg options and cold weather. I am a God-fearing man, so I love cows. I couldn't betray my vegetarian DNAs. It was hard to stick to my veggie instincts, but I was hopeful of the hardship paying off someday, somehow, somewhere. And just with that hope, I fasted for *Mahashivratri* relying only on chips for the whole day.

"Why don't you try Falafel or Tofu?" Some concerned white fellow could suggest to you. Falafel and Tofu are the only popular veg options in the UK. And not surprisingly, those items are also non-native. Falafel is a traditional Middle-East food item. It is prepared with chickpeas and a few other beans and served in the form of sandwiches and wraps. Tofu is a step-brother of paneer and should be treated like that only. It is prepared with soya milk and is protein-rich, but tastes poor. Something is better than nothing, and so these items rescue you from starvation and ultimately death.

"Hey, you know, it is illegal to die in the Houses of Parliament in Britain?" Varma shared his myth-fact-base.

"Oh, the easiest way of becoming immortal, isn't it? Just go and hide in the House. Well, if a person dies then is it legal to file a case on God? Are Brits atheists?"

Gowardhan's questions are unanswered till date.

Frustration and disappointment after lunch were visible on my poor face. One day, one Brit fellow came towards me in the office and asked what I had for lunch. Honest me told him. Talkative Indian in me told him the history too.

"Oh, so you are taking the same lunch in the same restaurant for consecutive days? Let me suggest something to you. Why don't you try the *street*? I guess it serves Indian also if you prefer."

London, and for that matter every developed city, has everything if you know where to look at.

"Thank you very much, John. I would die to visit the place." I was delighted, not only because of other cuisines I could get, but the *street* must be cheaper than posh restaurants. Saving is in the blood, always, and everywhere. I decided to run on the path shown by John. The next day, we were on the *street*, and John was quite right about it.

The *street* was soaked in the white fumes. All the hawkers were busy in producing fumes, making cutlery noises and creating some nuisance to give a feeling of more work done on the food, and ultimately that work getting converted into the great taste. On the streets, none of the hawkers seemed British. By now, we were decent enough to differentiate Brits from others.

"So, no Brit stall. The probability of getting satisfactory food is high." I guessed.

"Let's go get some fumes," Gowardhan suggested, and we went for a walk across the street. There were stalls of different cuisines- Indian, Arab, Spanish, Japanese and a lot more. There were boards with the descriptions. The more description was tattooed on the arms of the hawkers.

"Is that a sign to show the world they are badass?" Gowardhan questioned the motto of getting the whole arm tattooed.

"Maybe. Different regions and their modes of showing the badass-ness."

We wandered the whole street and neatly observed the menu cards, and that made me wonder. My notion about the street being cheaper was fictitious. There was hardly any difference. We wanted to investigate whether at least in taste was there any difference.

We stumbled upon a counter whose board read-
Biryani. The board also read *Veg-Biryani.*

"Although their spelling of Biryani seems incorrect, their intentions are good. Look, there is veg-biryani available."

The vendor did not look Indian by any standard. I just hoped Biryani would. I was asked about the size-Small, Medium or Large. I opted for Medium. My whole life I have been mediocre; medium is on my mind, then and always.

"What options do you want?" A man in his early forties was asking me in his strong Arabic accent. It was difficult to interpret his accent and also his intentions. What options can a veg-biryani have?

"Sorry?"

"Which curry? Which curry?" He asked repeatedly and pointed towards the round vessels. I tried to hop into them, and he started opening one by one. There were three. All looked dull, but I had to choose one.

"That one please," I said.

"Just a moment." He said and started preparing.

"Want a sweet curry?"

"No."

"Want *pappad?*"

"Yes."

"Here it is. Fifty more pence, please." He asked, offering me the box.

I had no choice, but to accept the *papad* for half a pound. I started respecting *papad*. We should not take anyone for granted; everything has a value.

Biryani was better than most of the veg items but a bit oily. That made my abdomen roar.

"You don't have a powerful digestive system it seems. With little oil, your bowels are resigning." Gowardhan ridiculed.

It made me silent, but not my stomach.

Life is a trade-off, full of compromises. If you want to please your tongue, it turns the stomach off. You cannot make everyone happy, that's the rule of life. It's just about preferences and priorities, and unknowingly for me, my tongue surpassed my stomach.

***

In western countries, there is a tradition followed in most of the offices that employers arrange lunch every Friday for their employees. That's a nice idea and we should copy this practice like most of their cultural norms. Fortunately, our London office too followed that tradition helping us to save a few more pounds, and supposedly a good amount of Indian rupees. We were eager to experience how these Brits mingle with each other, crack jokes and have lunch together because they are often blamed to be self-centered.

Now, ordering food for vegetarians was not a simple job as it is in India. In India, it is pretty simple and obvious for vegetarians - Paneer is the saviour. Our menus are not at all complicated. There are sections-Veg and Non-veg and our dish names are self-explanatory. If there is a chicken, the name starts with chicken, if mutton, with mutton, if paneer, with paneer — simple and clear. But western menus don't like simple and clear things; they make them complicated to confuse you more. This confusion is more than you have for deciding between paneer tikka masala and paneer butter masala. First, they don't classify vegetarian and non-vegetarian dishes. How much time and space would be required to put red or green dots anyway? Second, they use fancy names even for vegetarian dishes that make you suspicious and double check whether everything is vegetarian in it. The next one is, you hardly have an idea what and how the food will be.

With stalking dishes over the internet, we ordered the food based on their looks. Now, when the food gets delivered to the office, you imagine everyone will rush happily to have lunch together. But it doesn't happen. Queue-loving Brits won't rush for anything, let that be futile free food.

Chronologically, this happens thereafter - people get up from their desk. Take their food; they won't peep in other people's food boxes. Self-centered people do not care for other self-centered people. Come to their desk again. Open the box and start the lunch. You surprisingly watch them, but they are not watching you back, they are just watching the monitor and the food. In India, except for the loo, we invite people to every activity. Few people invite for the loo too. People mind if someone refuses to join them and that is considered suspicious. Going together is important for us, and we mind if people turn away from that. Having food together is an important aspect of our lives. We hardly indulge in having food alone. The main reason is Indians don't mind sharing the food. So, even if you don't like your food but like someone else's food, you are good.

"Westerners don't share anything it seems," Gowardhan asked for a debate.

"They share happiness." Varma jumped into it.

"And wives." Gowardhan's old habit of nudging.

"It shows your cheap mentality."

"It shows your lack of sense of humour and inability to identify exaggeration."

"It's not like-" and Varma stopped as he saw Harry coming. He was coming with his food-box. Gowardhan asked Harry-

"Hey Hari, got your food?"

"Yeah, I guess so," Harry said looking at the sticker of his name on his box.

"Is mine there?" Gowardhan asked further. Indians want to talk and they can't suppress that emotion.

"I guess so if you had ordered" Harry replied cunningly.

"Of course, yes. Okay, then I'll get my food and come. So, where are we sitting?"

"Me at my place and you at yours I guess," Harry said, not looking at anyone, but at his food. Gowardhan was puzzled.

"Hey guys, I'm starving. Enjoy" Harry vanished within a few seconds.

"This is utter nonsense. What is the point of throwing a free lunch then? To save a few pounds of employees?" Gowardhan was not amused by the idea.

"What? Why are you looking at me? Are you guys joining me or you too want to eat garbage in front of your monitor?" He fumed.

***

We love to invite people to our home, even if it's not our country and not our home. We get that immense pleasure out of their satisfaction, especially if they enjoy the food. It is ironic to go to someone else's country as a guest and become a host there and invite the actual hosts as the guests. It's in our blood, can't help it. We too invited some close company colleagues for dinner one evening. They were shocked, of course, because it is not a common practice to invite people at home in western countries. They may invite you for the drinks outside, but hardly to their homes.

On the other hand, Indians put their privacy at stake and invite guests. They feed them and force them to live at their place, and this is irrespective of the family's financial condition. Often hosts make their bedroom available by adjusting themselves to the other rooms, or in the kitchen if the case we are considering is from Mumbai.

So, those shocked colleagues came, but not empty-handed, they came up with a costly petal lily bouquet. We all just hoped they could have bought the money instead. Do bouquets have a return policy?

Red-faced colleagues after having the spicy dinner seemed extremely happy. They termed Indian cuisine as the best in the hope that they would get an invitation again. We could easily sense the liars. It was around midnight, and they were upset about the fact that they would miss the long sound sleep. Brits are very particular about their sleep cycle. One of them revealed he had sleepless nights during his graduation days and it was cumbersome. We Indians don't have a problem with that. We have thousands of call centers who shuffle your nights into days and make you strong psychologically. Our student community is known for no-sleep-night in the exam season. We even had a character in Ramayana - Kumbhakarna who used to sleep for half of the year and remain awake for the rest. He is an epitome of sleep-extremism.

"Oh God! I won't get enough sleep. Must be a tough day tomorrow." Harry imagined.

"Take sick leave then." Gowardhan had a solution.

Recommending this was just a conversation initiator; all we wanted to know was their leave policy.

"So, how many sick leaves do you get?" Gowardhan who failed to stab the urge asked immediately.

"Sorry, sick leaves? What do you mean? I did not understand."

"I mean, how many times you can be ill and bunk the office?" Straight to the point Gowardhan was.

"Oh," Harry giggled. "This does not make sense. Sorry, but, how can you tell this beforehand? We take leave whenever we feel sick, and that's it."

"So, there is no limit on the sick leaves?" The puzzled look on Gowardhan's face and deep envious disappointment on our faces.

"No! You can take leaves whenever you are sick. I mean - why does anyone want to welcome a sick person in the office? Wait! But, why are you asking this, and why are you so surprised? Is the case in India different?"

"We have fixed, limited sick leaves in India."

Now, the Brit was surprised.

"I'll tell you a secret. In India, when we are not sick, we take sick leave. And when we are sick, we often come to the office. We even have this innovative concept of 'planned sick leaves.' We say- 'I'm taking sick leave on coming Monday', and that is not surprising for others."

Harry couldn't suppress his laughter. "Holy shit" he screamed.

"And even if you take sick leave when you are sick; you'll not be believed the next day. Your colleagues will ask you - So, how was the long weekend? What did you do? And if you tell them you were in bed the whole weekend, they will wink and ask - With whom?"

***

One of the best things about the IT industry is team lunch. Team lunches are so judgmental that the company's reputation and its performance is measured by the place chosen for the team lunch. No wonder to boast the super-coolness, startups arrange extravagant team lunches or outings, although they're bankrupt and their investors are behind them all the time. But these startups too have a point. They enjoy their lunch as if that's their last team lunch, which gets real in most of the cases. These IT companies actualize the common man's dream of high-class deluxe dining, and that's why common people adore these companies. This epidemic of arranging quarterly outings boosted the hotel industry in metropolitans in India. You see a coarse grassland outside of a city and after six months, you are going to the resort built on that grassland. Besides a luxurious meal, team outings are important as it gives the opportunity to interact with teammates, bash at their manager and office politics, gossip about the office couples, and post pictures to show how IT life is so eventful.

When will you curse your luck?

When you feel sick on the day of the team lunch!

Our manager arranged the team lunch as per the tradition.

"Hoya! Guys, what do you wanna have? Indian, Italian, Chinese?" One fine day he asked. "Or Pakistani?"

He winked and chuckled. "Or Bangladesi?" He laughed hard.

"Yeah, nothing specific. Anything which you think is fine", we all smiled with a lame response.

"Okay, then. There is this beautiful Italian restaurant in the next block. My wife likes it too much. So, what we can do is- we can skip that and go to the next Spanish restaurant."

We all laughed and agreed as we didn't have any other option. Who will counter argue the manager?

"Holla! Vamonos!!" He excitedly shouted at our desk so loud that the next two teams too got the idea we were going for a Spanish lunch.

"Another thing besides choosing that restaurant is, it is so near that I need not take my car. My wife loves driving, and she is a terrific driver. I let you imagine yourselves the meaning of terrific here, but to give you a hint as you are my friends, I'm afraid to sit beside her while she drives. She drives me crazy though." He continuously laughed for a minute.

"I think it's his all-time scripted joke," Gowardhan whispered in my ear. "And might be, just because to throw these lines which he thinks are funny enough, he takes everyone to the same restaurant." He continued.

We started rolling the eyes as we were looking at the menu card. Leave aside knowing the items; we were unable to pronounce them. Before having a Spanish lunch, we knew too little about Spain. The things Indians knew about Spain are limited - Barcelona, Tomatina and it is a tourist destination for a bachelor's party.

Now, during a team lunch, seating arrangement plays a big role. You curse your fate if you have to sit beside your manager because you can't concentrate on the food. You need to laugh and respond to his lame jokes and act as if you care. You miss the fun your colleagues are having sitting far away from the manager. I was that fateful person that eventful day.

"Sparkling water to me please," the manager ordered without waiting for anybody giving an indirect signal to stop talking and start ordering. Indian scene of ordering is easy as pie - starter, main course, dessert. But that day, I got to know, there is something you can order before the starter - sparkling water.

"Me too," I repeated to avoid pronouncing any other tongue-twisting item.

But my satisfaction of avoiding ordering the dish was short lived as the gorgeous waitress arrived to take the further order in no time. The manager again ordered instantaneously. Gowardhan was probably right. The manager was a frequent visitor and maybe just to crack *wife and car jokes*. The gorgeous waitress was looking at me with a pleasant smile. Her bright blue eyes were hoping me to order something expensive.

"Can I help you order?" She asked gently. The manager was looking helplessly with a missed opportunity.

"Sure. But something vegetarian." I responded.

"Aha! Green green!" She winked. "We do have Zarangollo Escali, a salad dish. Also with that, you can try Spanish Mollette" she continued in a typical Spanish accent.

"Also, we do have-"

"Yes, that's fine. Please take my order. The first dish." I interrupted. I knew I could not pronounce any of the dishes if I had listened to her further.

The order came after half an hour; a sizzling hot bowl full of steam and vegetables boiling inside. The decoration was overwhelming. There was more variety outside the dish than inside. I thought of waiting for everyone's orders to arrive but witnessed the manager munching his bacon peacefully as if there was no world left. I wanted to be the manager's favourite. I too grabbed the fork and started investigating on how to start my Zarangollo. On my fork there came unrecognized leaf. I put that hot thing into my mouth and felt nothing tasteful except it roasting my tongue. I took the second. The same result. To make it taste-worthy, I put everything available on the table. But that too failed. I looked sideways- my Indian friends were in similar conditions. I understood why Western farmers are rich. If you can sell leaves for such a high price, why wouldn't anyone become rich? Somehow we finished our dishes looking at the surrounding gorgeous people. On the way back we all were cursing the manager for his choice.

"His choice of food is the worst." Everyone agreed.

"And his wife's choice is double worst." Gowardhan's giggle turned into a scream.

Varma recalled an incident and told us to respect generous Brits.

"We respect all humans. All living species let alone English peeps." Gowardhan tickled him.

Fish and Chips is an all-time favourite meal in London. One day Varma was having it and he was asked if he was interested in taking a combo meal which serves coke and collectively costs less. Varma denied the combo and relied on the water he carried.

"Oh, so you showed your Indian saving mentality," Gowardhan commented.

He finished his meal and left. After a while, he was tempted to have coke, so again went and ordered a coke.

"And I handed him 2 pounds, to which he just asked 79 pence and not 159." Varma continued.

"Why? Because of your face?"

"He converted my previous order and coke into a combo meal. How generous and honest of him!" Varma told.

It was indeed a considerate and modest move. The honesty index for Brits in our mind has levelled up until I heard their rubbish claim.

"What?" I screamed and couldn't hold my laughter after Gowardhan told me he heard someone claiming *Chicken Tikka Masala* as British originated dish.

"I too don't believe that baseless claim. But you know, we are in their country and we should not irk them on their faces. So I just smiled, but my teeth were pierced in my lips due to anger."

It was such a fishy claim which the word *Masala* was enough to confirm. Brits can't even pronounce *Masala, leave* aside handling it in food. We Indians don't use water for any special reason. The equation is just simple - *masala* equal to India, spice heaven. Gowardhan and I, en masse, by and large, rejected their claim. The Brit honesty index levelled down.

"But, it is a disputed issue. Few claims that the dish originated in Britain when a Pakistani chef tried something and invented the dish." Procurator of Brits, Varma spoke.

"Even if we agree to you, tell me one thing - what is the origin of Pakistan? India. So whose dish is it?" Gowardhan applied the patriotic logic which no one should mess with.

"Okay, leave this aside, don't you agree tea is theirs?" Varma shifted his focus on tea.

"Tea is China's."

"But, who made it popular in the world?"

"Maybe Indians."

"No, British. The whole world agrees on that."

"You are not the whole world. Have you ever had their tea? No, you can't because it's not the real tea. To call their so-called beverage a tea is tea-shaming."

"It's not what you think, or I think, or any Indian thinks. It's what the world feels."

"Have you ever seen a Brit addicted to tea? Or for that matter tea stalls or people arranging tea-parties? The fact is - they don't love their tea. But, for us, tea is not just a beverage, it's a feeling. It's a character identifier - we judge people by the colour of their tea."

"That's stupid and childish."

"Okay. Close your eyes and tell me what comes to your mind, when I say - tea? I know, it's Assam. It's not Birmingham or Bristol, it's Assam, or at the max Munnar."

"Whatever you think. Tea is theirs. Period"

"Kohinoor is ours. Dot." Gowardhan rested his case.

Beer of Brits

"We crave for something more than our wives. Guess what it is." British manager was becoming too friendly with us.

"Neighbour's wife." Gowardhan was quick in dropping the bombshell.

Manager's eyes were on stalks. He couldn't believe what he heard. He was staggered.

"That's hilarious. Hands down." The manager laughed hard. "That was instantaneous, Gowardhan. Epic." He continued adjusting his jaws.

Gowardhan looked at me. He was gesturing what was so special in his comment. I half smiled. After all, such responses are commonplace in India.

"Okay, so I was asking you what's more dear to us. Anyway, as he already nailed it, I tell you myself - it's Beer. You give me a Beer, and I don't want anything more. We love Beer, and how much I can't tell you."

We smiled and nodded.

"So, we have a tradition here. We reserved Thursday as a Beer Day. Every Thursday, after office, we go for Beer. And this Thursday, you all are joining. You all are invited." The manager left, showing Gowardhan thumbs-up. Gowardhan acknowledged with a puffed chest.

"That's their spirit. They don't mind jokes about themselves, unlike we Indians. Just think how the Indian manager had reacted. Brits are a gem of self-deprecating humour." Varma was watching the episode from a distance. "So, are you guys joining this Thursday?" He asked, taking his hands off the pocket.

"Maybe. Let's see."

Alcohol is a significant part of the western culture, especially London's. Drinking is a cultural norm. And thus unsurprisingly, there is nothing strange or guiltier about following the drinking culture among people. Without drinks, there is hardly any meetup or outing. The customs and mythos of *drinks* are altogether different compared to the Indian analogue. It is a ritual in the UK. It is a mediator for social gatherings for them. But in India, drinking has a negative notion. Usually, it is a secret and anti-sacred event. The differences in this practice start from the invitation itself. In London, people decide time and venue and broadcast on their social circle. Other folks sometimes join with their families too. Or there is a day exclusively reserved for visiting a pub and carrying on the ritual. In India, we give invitations for drinks publicly usually not with words, but with the gestures we are famous for. Some of these gestures are- raising one eyebrow with a chuckle, winking, or just making eyes bigger. It is a matter of hearts, so words are not required.

India has temples in well-nigh every *chowk*. Likewise, the UK, particularly London, has pubs everywhere beautifully decorated with pristine flowers from the outside as if it's their house of worship. Maybe for them, it is. Pubs are the heart of the city, and people cannot live without them just like we Indian can't without worship places.

The pub is a public house which is licensed to sell liquor, its definition reads. I read this when I got confused after visiting one in London and then comparing it with the ones in India. In India - Bars, Discos, Clubs, and, Pubs are used as synonyms, but in the UK, they are not. You end up spending more if you make a wrong guess about them. In India, it is pretty simple - you want to drink, you want to enjoy music, you want to dance - you can visit anything - disco, club or pub. Often, the bar is linked to a restaurant, and so you'll not be allowed to dance there; but if the bar owner is in your acquaintances, you can also dance there. In the UK, it's peculiar and distinct. The pub is to go and drink but don't dance even if there is soft music. The club is to go, pay an entry fee, pay for beverages, but don't dance even if the music is live. Disco is to go, drink, and dance even if there is no music.

But out of all these, the pub is the one who gets the cheese. Pubs are people's favourite and can be spotted at every other corner. The 'serve' mechanism doesn't work there. You need to go to the counter, pay, and collect your drink there, all by yourself.

We too joined our colleagues on one such reserved Pub-Day. Again, why cross the manager?

***

"The weather is too cold today, isn't it?" Gowardhan asked, rubbing his palms just after we entered the pub cautiously observing it inside-out.

"I don't feel so. You're wearing a sweater. Still, you feel cold?" I asked

"I don't know about you, but I'm feeling cold." Dejected Gowardhan retorted.

"Maybe."

"Alcohol must cure."

"What do you mean? Do you want to drink?"

"Don't you?"

"No."

"Why not?"

"But why?"

"See, no one is judging you for taking one Beer here, okay?"

"It's not about the judgment people throw on. I don't want to drink, and thus not drinking. And I don't mind if you want to drink. I won't judge. I never judge." I exaggerated a little.

"I too don't want to drink. Just-"

"You just said you want to drink." I cut him in the middle.

"Okay, at that time I wanted to. But now, I don't."

"Don't talk like a kid, man."

Gowardhan went silent, looking outside a closed window until Harry arrived with a pint in his hand and excitement on his face. What's so special about Beer that lights up the people?

"Hey guys, why didn't you take anything? Come with me to the counter." Charged Harry wished.

"Harry, you please carry on. We will join you." I lied. We Indians never say, 'No' even if we are damn confident about it. Instead, we say - 'Let's see.' or 'You carry on. We'll join you sooner.'

We are such liars. So, if any Indian responds to you with such words - mark the response as No.

"Gowardhan, if you want to try out, please go ahead. Why do you want me to join you?"

"The fun is doing things together, you know?"

"That makes sense."

"Talk like an Indian." He shrugged. "You know what, we are again missing this opportunity. The opportunity that we couldn't get in India whatsoever."

"Which one? Drinking in the pub? Yeah, we won't be able to drink in London's pub when we are in India." I couldn't control my urge for long to blabber nonsense. Without a drop of alcohol, I was high. Does just the smell enough?

"The opportunity to have a great conversation with these people. With these British people being in their country. We should go and talk, know them better, and know their culture better. We should tell them about our things. Get to know about their better things." Gowardhan was breathless.

Did the surroundings make him sober? How could he be so rational and compelled?

"Yes, we should. Definitely. We should meet them more." and as I was about to praise him for his short one-liner speech, he muttered-

"Especially that bar girl."

"What? So, you want to try Beer because of her? You are pathetic. And call her a barmaid, and not a bar girl." I acted like Varma.

"Just look at her green eyes."

"Stop bullshitting, come to the point."

"Okay. Look how hot she is. How can I describe her? Have you ever seen such a girl selling liquor? Don't you want to try Beer for her?"

"Why do you need to take Beer for her? If you want to strike a conversation with her, you can order something else."

"And look like a kid?" Gowardhan finally expressed his concern. A concern of many Indians. The misconception is - If you don't drink, you're a kid. The more you drink, the manlier you are.

You have to be quick if you aim to hit on the barmaid or barman. You have to be in a queue as the pub is no exception for queuing. But don't be embarrassed to hit on the barmaid thinking the next person will listen to your pickup line. Because these queues are highly organized, and they keep a minimum of a full hand distance between the two so no one can listen to your pickup line.

"One more thing you need to bear in mind while hitting on is the selection of words. Brits may mean to your word selection. You can flirt with - 'May I get you a drink?' or even you can add 'This for me, and yourself?' after placing your order giving him/her a choice to have a drink on your account. Strictly you should not say - 'May I buy you a drink?' because they can perceive your offer as a charity. Even though 'buy' and 'get' have a similar impact, Brits get hurt by this. I wonder how they can find sense out of such similar words in the effect of alcohol. Similar with offering the food - while asking whether the person had the food, you should ask - 'Have you had your food?' and not 'Have you eaten your food?' Because pets 'eat' food, humans don't. They may get offended and this may trigger their sarcastic nerves. They can come up with, 'Ate? I'm not your pet, Sir. Excuse me.' Understood?" I overheard Harry lecturing Gowardhan and Varma together on the interesting topic of how to impress Beer selling Brits.

When I was busy with my thoughts of whether to agree with Gowardhan and grab the opportunity of observing the stunning beauty closely, someone was gently smiling at us.

"Hey, you guys did not take anything? Did not like the place?" Mr. Richardson, a soft-spoken respected figure, genuinely asked.

"Hey, hello. No no no. The place is perfect. Just we are confused about what to take." Gowardhan replied.

"Am I of any help?"

"The thing is, we don't drink. We are teetotallers." I simplified.

***

The fact that I'm a teetotaller is hard to believe for many, and I don't blame them considering the reputation of IITs and IT these days. But when your parents don't believe their ideal son in this non-ideal world, then that hurts. I can't forget those weird looks on my parent's faces and that nods whenever I come late. The moment when your parents stop asking- 'What did you do at the party?' with an innocent smile on their faces, you should understand they think you started drinking.

The problems faced by non-drinkers are genuine ones, but no one pays heed to it. In India, first of all, they are treated as kids and not grownups because isn't drinking the only sign of an adult? And not moustaches and beards? Or grey hairs which I have a lot? Or the bald patches I'm worried about? Or common sense? Well, but, no, you are a kiddo!

Also, there will be no event where you've not been forced to drink or at least taste. The only disadvantage I find by involving in alcohol-friendly places is extremely high-priced mocktails. If you don't take a mocktail, you are termed as stingy. Does it make sense to pay three hundred for a mere apple juice with a fancy name? Then some mischievous friends oath to trouble all the teetotallers. They come with an idea which proposes either you drink alcohol with them or split the bill equally even if you had just mocktail and they had every drink on the earth. You are termed stingy, miser, and unfriendly if you refuse to pay equally. This makes non-drinkers avoid going to such parties with lame excuses and for that these innocent non-drinkers are blamed as anti-social.

***

"Oh, I see. In that case, you can have mocktails or lemonades." Mr. Richardson suggested.

"Sure. Thank you. We'll join you in a couple of moments."

Some of the Brits may politely ask you, as usual, the reason for your choice of non-drinking and they seem genuinely interested to know the reason. Even if they are not, they won't show it. They won't laugh in between or change the subject when you are grossly explaining the reason why you don't drink. But the difficulty lies in making them understand the Indian culture and values, religion, family background, and such stuff which often shifts the party mood to the philosophical one which no one desires. That is imminent and obvious to happen if you are wandering glass-free in the pub.

"We should buy that." I pointed at souvenir Beer glasses with painted Beer in the Oxford Street store one day.

"Why? You liked them so much?" Asked Gowardhan.

"No. To use in the pubs to avoid philosophical discussions and explanations."

I can't pronounce the names of Indian mocktails correctly, so, pronouncing English mocktails was out of my scope. Gowardhan's condition was no different. Our aim was clear- the barmaid. We stood in the queue, just for her. Decided to spend money, just for her. Remembered good sentences to start the conversation, just for her.

It was my turn next. I ruined the startup line in my mind. With utmost courage, I asked-

"Hey, what do you have in non-alcoholic drinks?"
She answered softly, "Aha! We do have mocktails, lemonades, and sparkling water for you, Sir".

She seemed diligent from closer. I ordered lemonade. Who will waste money on water? Let it be regular or sparkling, does it matter?

"Sure, thank you," she said and got busy in the preparation. Her preparation included filling the ice-cubes in a glass, opening a bottle, spilling it and wearing a smile. The first sip and it reminded me- the lemon *sharbat* of India, but, a poor version of it. Like most of the western food items, London's lemonade was nowhere near India's *sharbat*.

Mind the gap

Local trains are called tubes in London. In those tubes if not anything, you'll listen to a crystal clear plummy voice instructing - 'Mind the gap.' The voice is so sharp and pleasing at the same time that it is the softest warning you'll ever come across. 'Mind the gap' is a trendy term in the UK and is the heart of the whole underground tube system. It is one of the Brit prides, and you can even get a souvenir of such.

"There is no need to warn about the gap here. Do you see any gap between the door and the platform? That's an unwanted super sophistication. Even if someone wants to fall into the gap, he has to struggle to fall into that." Gowardhan opined leaving the tube.

"There are some stations where the platform is a curved one; there, you can see the gap. Mind it." Varma explained.

"Oh, I am afraid. Next time when you see the gap, let me know. I'll mind it."

"I too feel that's over-cautious of them to announce as well as display it." I intervened watching the signboard of a man falling into the gap instructing- 'mind the gap.'

"Yeah, see, on the platforms too, you can see that written," Gowardhan added. "And tell me one thing. When everyone is busy with their headphones while leaving the tube, who you think is listening to the warning anyway. No one gives a damn. They mind to mind." He played with words.

"It's funny, but let me tell you one thing. UK folks get hurt due to tripping over their trousers, or laundry baskets, or just stairs. And in significant numbers. So, understand, these lame warnings are needed." Varma poured his internet search.

"Oh, then the warning makes sense." Gowardhan ridiculed.

"And one more thing you must not be knowing. This voice of the warning is too popular. But unfortunately, the man behind this voice died a few years ago. His wife is also a voice-over artist, and she too had given the voice for London tubes." Varma explained. "And I bet you guys. You'll badly miss this voice."

"But what's so special about it? We too have a PA system on our stations." Gowardhan wanted to see Varma angry.

"What? Indian railway PA systems? Those which address in at least three languages? Those who shut down at the most important time? Like, train number-two-one-three-eight-down, with two seconds gap in between every number, LTT Howrah Shatabdi express will depart from platform number- and the exact moment when it's going to broadcast the platform number, it gets shut off." Varma provided the exact version making us chuckle a bit.

***

If you are a television person, you must have watched those room and car freshener advertisements where the people are blindfolded and taken to the disgusting sites. And they are forced to guess what site it must be. People are seen enjoying the pleasant smell, take a wild guess, and say everything but that disgusting site. They may say it's the Bermuda triangle but will not say it's their kitchen. Similar will happen if you are blindfolded and taken to any tube station in London. It is soothingly silent throughout its operation. We were baffled to experience that. It is exactly opposite to ours.

London is surprisingly crowded, but not noisy. It was the rarest of the rare sight for us to witness calm and composed people waiting patiently for the train to arrive. They mind their own business, and they mind the gap too as instructed. They are often occupied with a book. Brits read a lot. A lot.

"Just they don't read about the British invasion history," Gowardhan muttered.

"They don't because that isn't available," Varma replied.

"What isn't available?"

"Their history of invasion."

"Seriously?"

"Yes."

"Next time we will bring our textbooks. Our history isn't complete without their history."

"Isn't there any UPSC type of exam?" I asked a sincere question.

They still stand with headphones, a bag, and a newspaper. I doubt if I can stand with such stillness even if I am being sketched. Couples kiss, but they kiss calmly. Couples hug, but they hug calmly. People know that even if they act agitated, that's not going to help for the train to arrive early. But in India, we become restless and look at our watches constantly with frustrating eyes as if the train arrives sooner because of that. Few folks peek bending themselves as hard as possible and constantly glare in the direction for the train to arrive early.

India is an adventurous country. You have to be adventurous on a daily basis. Getting into a local train is not less than an adventure.

"Grabbing a seat on Churchgate-Virar local is not less than hiking the Himalayas." My frustrated friend struggling on a daily basis to get out at Borivali confessed one day.

But that's not that difficult if you follow the unmentioned steps. You need to prepare yourself for the battle when you see the train in your visibility. The preliminary preparation includes keeping your spectacles in your bag safe, taking your bag in the front and going forward as close to tracks as you can. No matter where you are, you need to move forward and as soon as the train arrives, you should be close enough to kiss the man leaning from the door of the train. If you follow these guidelines, there are high chances of getting the entry. The experience teaches these steps better, so it's easy to identify a native person and a newcomer.

In London, you cannot guess that - all the people look the same per their behaviour on the platform. No one is in a rush. No one looks disappointed. Everything is just serene. Few don't even look at the train, they keep themselves busy in their own business of reading, listening to music, cuddling, kissing or simply in someone's arms. Staring at other humans is sparse. They are in their own world. I confirmed this when I gawked at everyone. They were busy in themselves and not staring at anyone. In between, I found someone staring at me. It was Gowardhan.

"But Indian locals are a step ahead than tubes. They are highly automatic." Varma surmised.

"In what sense?" Puzzled, I asked immediately.

"You just need to stand, you go inside automatically due to hundreds of people pushing you, and while getting out too, you just need to stand, and you get out automatically the same way."

"Yes, but occupying that position where everything happens automatically is critical."

"And scary. Stand at your own risk." Varma said, minding the little gap at Baker's Street.

***

One evening, we were rambling around the Notting Hills, a romantic part of London famous for its coffee shops and bookstores and Julia Roberts starrer Notting Hill movie. The evening was soothing, quiet, and blissful like most of the evenings of London. The roads looked deserted.

"Hey, what's up there?" Gowardhan tapped my shoulder. Few cars were standing one after the other. I glanced in that direction.

"Let's go there. I suspect an accident." I guessed.

The Indians couldn't resist peeking into other people's problems. Let it be a quarrel or an accident.

The next second, a light turned green, and cars moved at lightning speed.

"Oh, signal!" Gowardhan blew.

Signals were operating. And more importantly, people were following.

Who follows the signal on the empty roads without police officers? Do we? Brits do.

It was a frequent site to see buses, vans, taxis, cars, and pedestrians standing peacefully, waiting peacefully for the signal to turn green for them.

"This is so systematic. Just look at it." Varma said.

"What to look for? Those girls?" Gowardhan replied as we were crossing a clean road.

"Traffic. And people's traffic sense." Varma invented a new term. "Just look, how everyone follows the signals. Have you noticed any pedestrians following it?"

We kept mum.

"But does that help?" I opened my mouth.

"What doesn't help?"

"Their traffic sense? Even with their high traffic sense and ultra-sophistication, have you looked at their traffic jams?" I continued.

"What's with that?"

"Even though they follow the rules, there are the worst traffic jams. And then like in India, people get pissed off. Just they show it differently." I explained.

Not only just for proving Varma wrong but, London's traffic scene is really not any better than India's. Even with ultra-mannerism and sophistication, London roads are jam-packed at peak hours. And imagine how frustrating it must be for the driver to see all the organised mess around. Indian traffic jams are frustrating no doubt, but at least they are entertaining. People indulge in horn-honking competitions; few people try to sell things to you forcefully, few come and tie auspicious lemon-chili without your consent and a lot more. You can see bikers showing their stunts by making ways through the choked road where you thought even a bicycle couldn't fit. Also, pedestrians infiltrating the unorganised clutter of traffic on the road because the footpath is already occupied with those crazy bikers. There is always tensed-entertainment on the road.

"Varma, where do you prefer driving? In India or here?" I asked.

"Neither." He blurted.

Motorcyclists are rare on the UK roads due to the cold climate most of the time. Cars and buses you see all around. Driving a car on London streets is a tedious job altogether. First of all, it is not recommended to bark the horn unnecessarily. Secondly, you need to be calm and smile all the time, even though you are struck in steady still traffic. Thirdly, you need to maintain the safe distance with your neighbouring vehicles. It is a matter of self-control not to embed your car just behind the front car. We in India don't give anyone any personal space, let alone the space on the roads. No one leaves the space in between, and if you do, do not complain if any biker occupies that and the car behind you honks and abuses you for your sophistication. And lastly, you need to follow the signals in the UK. If it's red, it's RED; it's not orange - the mixture of red and green. There you don't have a choice, but to follow the signal. The only choice you have is to smile or not to smile.

"But they have limited choices of transportation, don't they?" Gowardhan said, observing an endless row of taxis one after the other.

"What do you mean? What else do you want?" Varma barked.

"Well, lesser than India."

"Excuse me?"

"Yes. We have one more option. Autos."

"Oh, so you love those autos who ask you to beg them in an uncivilised manner?"

"I'm just listing out the options. And do you know why we Indians are not fat like western people?"

"Please, enlighten me."

"Autos."

"What?"

"Have you seen the space inside? You have to be moderate to fit into that. Have you ever travelled in a shared auto? You have to be slim to be one of the fours. There is no space to be fat."

"So, overpopulation is a trait in disguise?"

"Do you guys know one more unique facility of us-motorcycle taxis?" I wanted to spread my knowledge.

"No. What's that? Seems like an oxymoron." The first time Varma was on the receiving end.

"I've seen that in Goa. There is the motorcyclist who acts as a one-person taxi. He will drive you anywhere in the city."

"That's unique."

"And innovative," Gowardhan added.

***

'Technology can be a part of the solution, as well as, can be a part of the problem' my IIT professor used to say. Although it seemed like a worldly statement and worked impressively in group discussions all the time, I never gave it a thought until I experienced such. 'Technology makes a gadget smart and man dumber' I postulated on similar lines. Sometimes, I wonder in the coming days, can technology replace the common sense? Or has this already been started? Maybe this is an exaggerated thought, but observing people, I don't think so.

London is confusing. They have narrow roads in the midst of the city, and secondly the street names are difficult to remember. Like Abbey Rise, 3 Valley Place, Abbott Street. And lastly, even if you remember the street name and ask out for help, your pronunciation can take you to a different place. To hell with all these petty problems, technocrats gifted ordinary people with technology-driven-Google Maps.

Google Maps is a mini oxygen cylinder for you in London. Google Maps knows all Abbeys, Valleys, and Abbotts. You need to put your destination location without spelling mistakes and follow the map instructions earnestly. 'Earnestly' I mean without any second thoughts or applying your common sense. If it says go straight 500m, you should go exact 500m no matter what comes in between, if comes a car, ask them gently to get away from your straight line, if comes a swimming pool, walk over the waters and so on, but don't waste your efforts in thinking what if the map is wrong. Technology can never be wrong, remember?

The Indian scenario of finding the location is different. Technology too has limitations when it comes to finding the address in between the narrow, precarious lanes. 'It is easier to read between the lines, but it's herculean to locate the address between the narrow lanes in Delhi' my Delhite philosophical friend used to say proudly. 'And I am damn sure Google Maps will take you to the different Paratha house if you try that in Chandni Chowk in old Delhi' he used to supplement. I completely agree with him after witnessing it myself in the lanes of Chandni

Chowk. Still, we need not worry about finding the address as we have a strong, guaranteed, and all time available solution, the people. Anywhere you go, you'll find people. If you don't find people, you are not in India. Indians get enthusiastic and energetic if you ask them the address except if you ask the address of some other medical shop in some medical store. Once I was trapped in perplexing lanes in Bangalore and wanted to visit the PCB repair store. Now, even if people don't know what PCB is, they can tell you the address of the store if you are smart enough to question them.

"Uncle, do you know where Manjunath Electricals is?"

"Manjunath Electricals?" He looked at me in disbelief as to how PG housing's name can be any electrical shop's name.

"I don't know," he said and started walking away. Maybe 'uncle' remark offended him. Maybe his bald head was a result of excessive roaming for software jobs.

"*Anna*, is there any electrical lane nearby?" I generalised my search query.

"Yes, there is. Go straight and second left", he instructed. The word 'Anna' made him appeased.

"Thanks, *Anna*," I said and thought it's over now.

"There will be a big garage. Go little ahead of that and take a right," stranger *Anna* continued.

"Thank you very much, *Anna*. I can find it from there."

"Yes, you can see it in the front there. But why are you coming here? It's costly here. Go to Yesvantpur market; you'll get cheaper."

"Thanks, *Anna*. Leave that. I'm not paying for this. My friend's work. Why worry about money then?" I winked.

"Oh, that's the case. Then fine." We both chuckled.

I learnt how a choice of words from Uncle to *Anna* changed the course of direction of help. 'Nice words make your half work done' the status of promoted software tester reads.

But a similar technique did not work in London. Once I had to take a different train route and I got out from a different direction. I knew I was nearby but didn't know exactly where. 'Why to take the phone out in this frigid weather and search for the address? Let's ask some Brit here' I thought.

"Excuse me," I said politely to a white passerby.

"Hey, yes please," he responded.

"Good morning. Um, can you please tell me where City Tower is?" I was still in my polite mode.

"Not really. But-" and he did what I could have done too. He pulled out his smartphone and started navigation.

"Sorry, but no great signal here. My app is stock-still." He confessed his failure to the technology failure.

In the meantime, I was observing him out of my Indian habit and explored his identity card. Within seconds, I knew in which company he worked and in what position. He was no longer a stranger. He was working in my neighbouring building. I found a way out. I asked him where his company location is, and found my way. He seemed proud of my intelligence.

***

Like everything else in the country, the buses too were posh and on-time. Unlike buses in India, there is no ticket collector inside. Even though the tube network is strong, buses play a vital role in transportation.

"It's just like our Mumbai." Gowardhan described the transportation network in London over the phone to his mother. On listening to his ear-splitting loud arguable proclamation, Varma turned towards me.

"Is he mad? How can he compare Mumbai's transportation with London's?"

I ignored his altercation with a smile and got busy in analysing the bus structure. Not to my surprise, the bus was too spacious and too clean, like all other UK things. At the entrance, besides the driver, you need to punch the card. And that's the ticket for it. You get out the next stop or the last one; the ticket remains the same. Surprisingly, the driver was not keeping a close eye whether people were punching for the ticket. He just listened to the beep sound coming after the punch.

"So, if you master the art of mimicking the sound of the beep, you can travel for free." Gowardhan came with a trick.

"First, master the art of responding to someone's hello." Varma slammed as Gowardhan didn't respond to the driver's greetings.

"What? The driver said hello to us?"

Varma ignored.

The bus was a double-decker and sufficiently empty. There was hardly a person at the top. I had a dream from my childhood to sit on the top floor of the bus. Brits don't have childhood dreams. Brits don't get fascinated by a double-decker. After some time, some

Brits who had double-decker dreams arrived on the top.

There was no part-time and full time job, loan schemes or NA plot advertisements that we always find in Indian buses. I felt pity for all the Brits who couldn't get those opportunities. Similar was the case with tubes. There were no expert advertisements inside. That reflects two things-either Brits do not suffer from sexual problems, or they don't have sexperts.

How the bus stops is vastly different from how it does in India. In a true sense, the bus never stops in India; it just slows down. Passengers need to adjust themselves and get out of the slow-paced bus. But, UK buses stop. And they stop for sufficient time to get down. In India, when the next stop is yours, you need to stand up from your seat, provided you had one. You need to be standing at the door to get down or jump when the bus gets slowed down. And if you don't follow this procedure, you have to face the wrath of the conductor, driver, and other passengers. In the UK, it was ferociously different. If the next stop is yours, you need to chill out. When the bus stops, you need to look out of the window to confirm if it's your stop. The driver then waits for passengers to get down. He then looks into the screen which displays what is happening on the top floor and then closely observes whether anyone is getting ready to get out. If he sees any movement, he again waits.

Waiting is in their blood. After he confirms all the people who wanted to get down are down, he slowly starts the bus. Slow and steady wins the heart.

"It looks as if no one is in a hurry here," Gowardhan said, observing a disabled man getting out of the bus in his wheelchair.

"That's because they leave on time so that they get on time." Replied Varma.

"Makes sense."

***

Westerners are hypersensitive about the things of terror horror. They are so sensitive that even if they listen to the related words, they will shit their pants.

"Remember this very carefully. No matter what, you should not say or even utter the blast-related words. If someone on the train listens to you saying-BOMB, they'll inform the police." Varma warned us before boarding a train to Scotland.

"And in our country, the popular topic of discussion in trains is Bomb-blast and terrorism." Gowardhan chuckled.

"Keep that discussion for some other day in India, okay?"

The train came exactly on time and left the station as per the schedule. The interior of a train was like a business class aeroplane. The chairs were better than my Boss had. There were huge and clean windows to enjoy the scenery. The air conditioner in the train was perfectly tuned to have the best possible atmosphere inside. The scene of lush green infinite fields, the grass-eating folk of sheep and cows, huge machinery and hardly any human was new to us. Little time after, a nicely dressed train-hostess came with a little canteen.

"Anything for you, Sir?" she politely asked with a shy smile and buoyant eyes.

"No, thank you," I replied, slightly making her disappointed.

"Thank you. Please enjoy the view." She excused herself with her non-sarcastic comment.

"Hot tea for me please." We heard Varma placing an order.

"And just yesterday he said - you can have tea in Indian Railways but not in the UK. And see now, he has resigned in front of beauty. Looks and colour are the unfair advantages anyone can have." Gowardhan expressed his concern.

"Let's start our eatery." I ignored his concern.

"Oh, yes," he said and pulled out a bag from his backpack containing yesterday's leftover. We had all one can ask for in a breakfast - sandwiches, cookies, and tea. As an Indian tea lover, we bought tea-packets all the way from India. Gowardhan found thermos in the house and so we were good. The train had a table for having food. Gowardhan bought paper cups from the office, and we were set to sip up the real tea. Varma had a look at our arrangements with expressions - 'Indians won't change.'
We wondered - where could we dump the garbage because the windows were locked and no one was littering on the floor. Just then I spotted something under the seat. It was a small dustbin, under every seat.

Too much tea makes human pee. The toilet was equipped with a big LED showing its status- VACANT in green and OCCUPIED in red. I went near the VACANT toilet and peeped in to ensure that it was empty. Technology cannot be 100% sure upon. I went inside thinking the sensors would understand that I got in. But software engineers like us must've forgotten to imagine this test case. The door was reluctant to close. I tried manually, but no luck.

'There must be something, look look look' I was hoping.

'If you search harder, you can even find God' my mind challenged my intelligence. Alas! I found one such button. I pressed it hard and slowly the door got closed. The status changed from VACANT to OCCUPIED inside too. I was relieved. I had my business done and got more relieved. A little technology geek in me aroused and I had a detailed look. The toilet was too big to be a toilet. The wash basin alongside the commode had touchscreen buttons for hot and cold water. The commode was accompanied with a stroll of two types of toilet paper. The freshener would make anyone stay there forever. I bet if you visit that toilet, you'll get your 'washroom-goals.'

After relaxing for five more minutes, I decided to change the status. I recommended Gowardhan to visit the place. For the next half an hour his chair beside me was empty.

Universal Happy Religion

The activity 'shopping' has no regional, cultural, geographical, and political boundaries. You go anywhere where humans are existent, especially women, you'll find the same enthusiastic, energetic, vigorous people involved in shopping. Shopping centers are the places with the most positive energy due to happy people. Although the nature of the shopping activity is different, people's love is universal.

The whole UK shopping system is contrasting to India's. So, if you plan to visit the shopping stores on Sunday evenings, well, be prepared to witness the closed shutters.

It's another shock to know most of the shops close by 6 PM on Sundays. And they are very particular about it. Like, you are outside the shop at say 6 and try to enter, you will not be allowed with apologies, of course. About 15 minutes before the planned closing, they will start shutting down the gadgets, switching off the lights, announcing the closure of the store. Don't wonder if you are asked to come the next day, even if you had shortlisted the items and just about to make the payment. We witnessed one such closure announcement in an electronic showroom as- 'The shop is being closed in a minute. Please carry out your further shopping from our online store.'

In India, the customer is a king. Still today. There is no concept of closure of a shop if a guaranteed customer is present. The shopkeeper hardly minds in keeping the store open till you make the payment. Thus, we have stores open even if you can see the shutter closed from outside. If you are living nearby college campus, the eateries are often open beyond midnight, beyond their limit. The timings displayed are for namesake just as the food items they show on their menus. This has happened many times when I visited a canteen and noticed the delicious items on the wall, ordered a few and the boy shook his head in denial.

"Then what do you have?" I asked angrily.

"Nothing from this list" he replied calmly.

The timings of the bistros are customizable as per the police raids. Small-scale vendors have an altogether different system irrespective of any time bound. It does not matter whether the shop is closed or the shutter is down, the shop serves all the time. There is a bell. You need to ring it unhesitantly. A small boy or a woman or a man or a dog will peep from the terrace, and ask you what you want. You'll get what you want. At any time. At every time. Indians have conquered the time as well.

***

There are a few skills you cannot boast about or make it official mentioning it on your resume even if you are proficient in them. In India, for that matter, flirting tops the chart followed by bargaining. Although flirting has some social recognition, it is 'bargaining' which is quite underrated. Indians are born bargainers and there should not be any strife about it. The unofficial survey results at the shopping centers at Sarojini Market in Delhi and Fashion Street in Mumbai claims that there is an excessive secretion of this bargain-hormone in women.

"Women are bargain-machines. If you sell a product at Rs. 100 to a man, take my word - if you can sell the same product to a woman at Rs.80, you are a winner." said a popular Bhaiya on the Fashion Street.

"What is the 'see-to-buy' ratio?" Someone asked.

"It's different. Here, for men, it's 60-40, but for women, it's 90-10 and, touch wood, it's great." He continued.

"It's not uncommon for a woman to ask to show her everything in the store and still she refuses to buy and go to the next store for the same products and the same process follows. But we don't mind. It's expected. We are habitual." His subordinate Chotu added.

Negotiation, a sophisticated term for bargaining, is now not a monopoly of recruiters. Bargaining has entered every field. It is a basic human right, and people use this right rightfully from time to time. The happiness of successfully applying this skill is unbounded. Bargaining is in the blood of the Indians, and it's difficult to segregate; doesn't matter if you have become rich.

'What rich? Rich women are the ones who do much khich-khich bargain while deciding our salary. Even we don't do that much for saving such a small amount.' You must have heard this statement of several gossip-queen housemaids.

"The only competition for us in case of bargaining is from Chinese," Varma remembered his Hong Kong visit. "That's why our border is facing a serious threat. Sometimes, people forget what to bargain and where to bargain." He continued.

"But it's ours, and will be ours." Gowardhan's chest bulged.

"Of course." Varma showed his patriotism.

With great bargaining comes great consensual lies. We Indians lie. We are speaking the truth here. Customers lie despite knowing that the vendor knows it. But this is mutual. For our lie, vendors too lie in return. This is an unsaid agreement both parties sign.

'We are your regular customer.' followed by 'We know that madam.'

'Last week only, we bought two kurtis from you.' followed by 'That's why we are offering you such a low price, madam.'

'Last week, you said you'd cut the price next time.' followed by 'Yes, madam, you go anywhere, you won't get this price, madam. Take it and go, madam.'

'Okay. Not yours, not mine. Final it for 250.' followed by 'Okay madam. Only for you as you are our regular customer, madam. Please, don't tell others that I gave it at such a low price. Visit again, madam.' and so on.

Both the parties are well aware of the fat lie thrown at each other, but those are well perceived and only help in building the business. And as far as lies which makes both the parties happy, they are good lies. Lie, but lie for good — a lesson to learn for others.

People going abroad have to fulfil the mandatory duty of getting something for everyone in their close acquaintance. As soon as people get to know you are the lucky one to go abroad and have some fun, they too want some share of it. Before you make any plans, their plans are ready. Before you list down what to buy, their list is already conveyed to you. 'Don't promise when you are happy and don't reply when you are sad' a proverb says.

You realise the truthfulness of the first part when you try to accommodate all the things while leaving the foreign country. You become a temporary celebrity- before going abroad and after coming from abroad. People cajole you for their things to buy from foreign. Sometimes, there is no problem bringing a few things that are demanded, but it is unclear whether they expect it as a gift or they will sportingly hand over the money. The never published blog of onsiters says, 'It is observed that 90% expect it as a gift.' One of the bloggers reported on the condition of not being named - 'for the managers, it is 98%.' This un-clarity affects your selection. If the girl is willing to pay and make that clear, you go for - Guess, Kepler, Gucci or Armani, but what if you are not clarified and kept in a dilemma? Then you do a simple thing - you go to the local shop - select something that looks like a handbag and removes the price tag. The heart pains when the girl says on your face - 'What's this shit? We get thousand-time beautiful handbags here.' Few express the desire to pay but make you a salesman. What do they want from you? Pictures of everything in the showroom.

Mr Sitharaman achieved the height of stupidity when he clicked pictures of iPhone 7- 32 GB and 128 GB, and sent it to Mrs Sitharaman.

Few smart people remind you from time to time so that you shouldn't forget their things, but, the way they do that is clingy. The people who never initiate the conversation are now asking about your whereabouts.

She: Hey dude, how are things?

Me: Hi. I'm doing good. How are you?

She: Bored. What do you expect from this office? You know how boring it is. But, I hope you must be enjoying it there.

Me: Haha. Yeah, sort of.

She: Hey, did you get the chance to look for my handbags? Hidesign or Cathy? Don't tell me you didn't. I will kill you if you come empty-handed.

But there are a few girls who don't have any hidden intentions and still make a fool out of you. They are your sisters. They don't request. They command. You can't say you don't have time. You have to make time.

You are not allowed to forget any of the things they demanded. You only have the liberty to forget the things you planned for yourself.

"Get me one magenta purse". My sister ordered.

"Okay. Send me some pics so I'll find something similar."

She sent a few links. I wondered why she didn't order from those online stores in the first place. But, I'm bound not to ask such questions. I wandered and lost hunting for her purse. Finally, I found one, fortunately. I was delighted.

"Look, exactly what you sent." I sent the picture.

"That's not magenta."

"That is."

"No."

"I can see with my eyes."

"Okay, take it at your own risk. If not magenta, the consequences are yours."

That day, I understood why girls easily solve those find-the-difference puzzles.

"Keep one very important thing in your mind for good. If you get any cheap clothing from here, don't forget to tear off the tag from it." Mr Sitharaman suggested when he was taking off the tag from the top he had bought for his wife.

"Why so? It signifies size, right?" I asked, failing to get the intention.

"With size, there is something more written on it. Made in-"

"What's the harm in keeping it anyway?"

"Who will believe you that you bought from London when they see Made in Bangladesh on it?"

"Oh, is that the scene? I never paid attention to that. Just let me have a look." I went to my room and duly checked the tags.

Made in India. Removed.

Made in Bangladesh. Removed.

Made in the UK. Happily retained.

Made in China. Removed.

"You are a saviour. You truly are." I paid gratitude to Mr Sitharaman for saving me from the Tsunami at home.

***

Weekend evenings are reserved for shopping in India. With ever increasing shopping malls, manipulating offers, handy money, and unnecessary requirements, you can hardly find any such destination scarce. It is always full of lively people. Going for shopping and buying something is not the same. Big online players and their click-to-delivery systems are taking up the pace. Window shopping is a hobby that is picking up rapidly. Despite all this, going to a store and spending time there is a different fun altogether.

"Window shopping is enjoyable. That requires no money to pursue anyway" Gowardhan stated one evening when we were roaming in search of discount offers at Westfield, London.

"But, what about the time wasted?" I argued.

"Didn't you read the famous quote - The time you enjoy wasting is not wasted?"

***

Honesty is the best policy people say. But in this era, does it hold well enough, especially in sales and marketing? I was buying a shirt at a London outlet, and it was bright blue. As a colour conscious Indian, I asked the saleswoman gently,

"Would it leave its colour after the first wash?" This is such a typical question in India as far as bright clothes are on the tables.

My question made her numb. She excused herself and went to her manager. Her manager within a minute came running and told me-

"Sorry Sir, but, I doubt it can hold on a colour for every type of wash. I mean for a gentle, detergent wash, it can hold, but not sure whether with other washing settings." I did not understand what settings she was talking about. I asked her because I need to convey these instructions to our Mavshi who anyway ignores whatever I instruct. I felt pity about the sales girl that she needs to run to her manager for such a minor doubt. Come to India, and you'll never be directed to higher authority unless it's for the payment or bargaining. You ask anything, the salesperson has a perfect convincing response to that. You wear anything, they will praise you. If you doubt about the material of the clothing whether it's cotton or synthetic, depending upon your doubt, they have the response. If you want synthetic, they will say-

'No Sir, it's not cotton. Touch it, touch it and you'll understand. Cotton doesn't come like this. Cotton is damn thin. It's like you can use it as a tea stirrer. Heheheheh.'

On the other way round, if you doubt whether it's cotton, they will say-

'It's 100% Cotton, Sir. Touch it, touch it. Oh, I know why you are doubting. You've seen the polyester cotton, that must be duplicated one. This is original. It is soft like silk. Touch it, touch it. Feel it, feel it.'

If you doubt whether it will fit because it looks smaller, they will say-

'Sir, it's cotton. After the first wash, it will expand and will fit on you. Don't worry!'

And if you doubt because of its larger size, they will say-

'Sir, it's cotton. After the first wash, it will contract and will fit on you. Don't worry!'

I don't understand how the cotton understands when to contract and when to expand. People don't know when to contract and when to expand and in front of whom, but Indian cotton does.

***

"What is happiness, according to you?" I asked. I was in a philosophical mood.

"Getting my haircut from the soft hands of a Blonde" Gowardhan uttered, watching straight into the saloon. I never saw Gowardhan so concentrated.

"I am serious. Tell me." I asked again, joining Gowardhan in his activity of under-the-hood stalking. He said-

"I'm extremely serious about this. To me, happiness at this moment is getting a haircut from that Blonde." He repeated his stance looking at her more intensely. "Look, opportunity knocks the door once, twice but not thrice. What I want to say is," and he paused to take a fierce glance and continued, "Now, you have an opportunity to let that girl touch your hair. Hairs on the head, okay?" I was expecting the last part. "Probably next time too you can get a chance to visit the UK and come to this place, but you never know whether you will get a third chance. Also, the probability of that blonde leaving this job is higher."

"That's highly rubbish." I don't know what made him come to such a ridiculous analysis. No wonder the poor man was always rejected and becoming an analyst is still his distant dream.

"But, the day we left India, the last thing you did as I remember is getting a haircut. You are the one who did the math and told us how getting a haircut is a costly affair here. And now, just because you spotted her, you want a haircut?" I made my point.

"To make my answer short - YES. And I'm in no mood to ruin my mood further. If you want to come, come. I'm going after she finishes with her client. Otherwise, I may get assigned to that Fatso." He winked. The excitement was clearly visible in his other eye. I joined him as soon as I made my mind on another Blonde. I was happy from the inside on the thought of getting a feel of the soft hands of Blonde on my rough hairs, but I was not showing my happiness and cursing Gowardhan for wasting money. That's a genuine human emotion. They want something, but they want someone else to make efforts on their behalf for getting that thing. I envy Gowardhan sometimes. He always chooses his happiness leaving aside the social obligations.

After checking sufficient cash in our pocket and taking God's name to make us successful in our mission, we entered the saloon.

"Hello gentlemen, how is sunny London treating you?" A middle-aged white lady welcomed us with a big grin and pleading eyes. She offered us a seat. We both turned back and took a glance to confirm if she welcomed us and called us 'gentlemen.' It was rare for us. In response, we synchronously said - "Good" and sat on the couch.

"At least, we should have greeted her in response," I told Gowardhan.

"What happened to your choice? Don't get distracted from the target. Concentrate on the prey. And pray." he replied.

When I inspected the saloon, it looked more like a furniture store. Despite that being a saloon, there were hardly any hairs on the floor. There was no noise - UK scissors too don't make noise, unlike Indian scissors. All the activities were going slow, smooth, and steady. No one looked in a hurry, neither customer nor barbers. I remember my usual saloon in India which is never quiet; it is all noisy. Healthy discussions happen on various topics ranging from Bollywood to Politics. Opinions flow from how a particular actor should have raised his son to why the current government can lose the next election. These discussions are inevitable. Indian barbers are all-rounders. They engage customers in usual talks, they listen to other conversations, take an active part in them, also watch television when their favourite scene comes and yes, cut the hairs too. All this one at the same time. Indian saloons are crowded places, especially if you visit it on a Sunday morning. You may need to wait for an hour, but the entertainment is guaranteed. This waiting time can increase if you are a kid not accompanied by an elder. There are no queues. There is a referral as well as an acquaintance system. If you are familiar with a barber, the chances of you surpassing others and getting the seat are higher. If you are not, you remain a spectator and watch people come after you and get their work done.

When I looked at the lady in the London saloon who welcomed us, I remembered my barber. A bald, generous, sociable man. When I started going to the saloon on my own, I was often asked to sit for a long time because in everyone's eyes, I had no urgent business to do and there was no harm in wasting my time. One fine Sunday, I was done with the waiting. I was running out of patience. I shouted-

"What is this? I'm waiting here for so long you all know. This man came after me and you took him before me."

"Beta, he came before you actually. He had some work, beta. He went to work, and now he came back," my barber uncle lied.

"Haha! As if I'm new here" I refused to accept.

"Don't be impatient. Next is you. Just give me another ten minutes and then you. Today, you'll have the best haircut. Your friends will ask you from where you got it done. Tell them my name. And even if they come here before you, I'll take you before them." Uncle was trying hard to calm me down. Indian barbers outsmart their customer retention policy. IT management should learn from them.

"I'm done here. I'm going." I refused.

"No, no, I'm not letting you go. Next is you, beta."

"I'm done and done. I want to go home or some other saloon."

"Now, I want just five minutes and next is you." I saw no way to go out.

"Let me go outside. I want to pee badly." I lied.

"Okay, pee here, but don't go," said uncle and joined his hands to make a hand-vessel.

Gowardhan pinched me - "Hurry dude. Otherwise, you'll be the prey of that monster," he pointed at the horrifying bully-like figure. Only because of his dress-code, he seemed to be one of the barbers. We both were just worried that our Blondes should not be allotted to others. Fortunately, our prayers were heard. Happily, we sat on the fluffy hot chair. I experienced the rare emotion - excited and nervous at the same time.

"Hi! I'm Kate", said the cute Blonde offering a handshake. I accepted the handshake with shaking hands. I had never heard such a soft voice before. I had never touched such smooth skin before. I had never eye-contracted such pupils before.

"Hi! I'm good," I presented my how-are-you-doing response. "How are you doing, Kate?" I asked further. I don't know from where I got such confidence. If I had such confidence during my teen years, I would have had my own Kate.

"I'm doing perfectly fine. Thank you very much." Kate was highly delighted.

"Which colour do you like, Sir?"

Which colour was she asking about? Of what? Are these Brits so frank and forward? Different thoughts on a generic question buzzed my mind. I acted sober.

"I like grey," I answered, hoping to be different and unique.

"But we don't have that colour, Sir. Choose between these, please." She showed me hair-cutting gowns of different colors. I chose Black. To my right, I saw Gowardhan draped in Saffron. Kate took a minute to set the chair and instruments up. At that exact moment, my mind was imagining how my mother and Kate would live in peace. I was deeply tensed about how Kate would walk in my village farm after the rains. I was wondering what our children would look like- like a Zebra?

"How about this?" Kate started the hand-shower and asked for my compliance, which snatched me away from my sweet imagination.

"Perfect." I nodded.

A hair bath before cutting them down was new to me. It was as if we offer water to slaughtering animals before slaughtering them. Kate's fingers were all around my head. I wish time could stop everything excluding Kate's fingers running through my head.

"Just a moment. I'll be back in a minute." She went to take some not-so-known things.

I took a glance at the whole saloon. If that much space had available in India, we could have a salon, a tea stall, and a watch repair shop. On another chair, I saw a kid accompanied by his mother. He was calm and quiet as if on the drugs. I don't remember me or any child of my age then not crying loudly. Sophistication affects badly. Then I glimpsed at Gowardhan. He had shut his eyes, must be for a better feeling. From his expressions, it was evident he had hairgosm in his imagination. At least he was optimizing his money by imaginative enjoyment. I shut my eyes in that hope.

***

The first weekend in London we spent in Stratford looking savagely for winter jackets. The policy was simple - if they are cheaper than the price in India, our relatives have no option but to accept jackets even though they could be out of size and they could practically be unusable in India due to the Indian climate and thickness of the jacket. Our initial two hours went in just shortlisting the stores with huge discounts.

"I know how it works. It is the same everywhere. They will increase the price by 20%, and then decrease it by 20% on one particular day claiming it to be 'SALE.' So manipulative." Gowardhan whined.

"That's not the case. They don't involve in such cheap gimmicks. These are real discounts just like Black Friday deals in the US. You come tomorrow; you shall witness the higher price, the original price." Varma opposed.

"Well, anyway, we can't afford to come tomorrow. So, let's not argue and buy if we find something reasonable." I interrupted.

The countries with lesser population densities have this advantage- their change rooms in malls are mostly available. Grabbing this opportunity we spent huge time trying everything imagining the physiques of our brothers, and shortlisted jackets for them and for ourselves. As soon as we looked at the price tag, our brain automatically multiplied the price by 85 and was ready with the Indian price. Our brains knew where to invest its intelligence. Mathematical skills and Indians, you see!

"Where did you get that from?" One gallant dandy man was asking me, standing one rack away, watching at the jacket I was holding. My face instantly lightened seeing an Indian in London. I don't understand what made me happy interacting with an Indian, whereas in India when there were thousands of Indians around all the time didn't amuse me anytime. But in London, seeing one Indian made me peppy.

"Yes, from there." I pointed the finger in the right direction. "Behind those handbags." I continued.

I don't like to converse in English with Indians who can speak Hindi. But, as he started in English in the first place despite knowing I was too an Indian, I couldn't let my ego down. I continued in English.

"At what price?" Typical Indian in him woke up and directly jumped on the point.

"It's cheaper. Just 11 pounds. Around a thousand rupees. Last piece of M size. I'm afraid if there are any left now."

"Oh, it's quite cheap actually."

"Today is a sale. If you come tomorrow, you may find it at a higher price without a discount." I believed in Varma.

"Yes, I know." He confirmed Varma.

"In India also, we get these types of jackets. But, you know, as it would be from London, this jacket would gain more respect. We, Indians, you know." Typical Indian in me was extending the conversation.

"I can understand." He chuckled. "Okay, thanks. I'll check there. It's there right?" He pointed at the exact direction.

"Yes, there. Behind those handbags."

"Thanks. Where are you from?" He asked casually and was about to leave in pursuit of the cheaper jacket.

"Mumbai. And you? Delhi?" I guessed faintly of his origin with his Delhi-cut beard and fair colour.

"Lahore." He said and smirked.

We exchanged a half smile with 'It's okay and let's not make it awkward' look on our faces. Waving a hand and the understanding signals we parted our ways — my first encounter with Pakistani.

***

"I've got an idea to end the India-Pakistan tensions." I proposed a solution after detailing out this Delhi-Lahore incident that night.

"What's that?" Asked Gowardhan trying to fit in an oversized jacket.

"Why the hell did you buy a jacket of double of your size?" Varma neglected my peace solution and concentrated on Gowardhan's jacket. I understood-peace was not the priority for Varma and for most of the politicians.

"It's a 70% discount, and so in the excitement, I didn't try there. Anyway, I'll give this to Pramod Bhaiya. It would be perfect for him. Or to Manoher or simply to my father. Someone will fit in it." Gowardhan explained. "Okay, what's your solution?" He turned toward me.

"Discount sales across the border. No one will mind. Divided by partition, united by discount sales. How's it?"

"Bullshit," Varma shouted and left the battleground.

Koh-i-noor

British colonisation is an imperative part of Indian history. Due to its cause-effects taught in history syllabus, Indians are well aware of it. Even after 75 years of independence, we have a sporting-grudge, if such a term exists, on British. And the funny part is, British people don't know anything about it. Partly because they ruled over more than half of the world, so, if they include this all in their history syllabus, students need to study till old-age. Neither are they interested in letting their people know what their ancestors had done.

More than anything, the dearest thing Indians could not hold their peace on is the claim that the British took away the Kohinoor diamond forcefully. Was it a gift? Was that an act of theft? No one is completely sure. But one thing every Indian is sure of is- Kohinoor is dear to us even though we don't know why it's so precious and what's its history, but we are curious and yet envious. The precious diamond is conserved in the Tower of London. Visiting London and not visiting the Tower of London to have a look of the beauty is an immense crime no Indian shall commit. To avoid the pretentious question 'How does the real Kohinoor look?', we decided to visit the Tower.

London is one of the most visited tourist places in the World. To have a statistical record, often at the attraction, visitors are asked about their origin country. London is strikingly costly for tourists. The entry fees are sky touching. And there is this unusual custom of offering tickets with donations and without donations. The Tower of London is no exception to that.

"If you add the ticket price with donations, we could get a nice holiday package in that amount in India" Gowardhan uttered standing in a queue.

"Two tickets, please." I requested at the counter.

"Which country, Sir?" the lady at the counter inquired.

"India," I told, confidently and proudly. After all, ethically Kohinoor belongs to us, maybe.

"With donations or without donations, Sir?" the lady at the counter was doing her job.

"No thanks. Without a donation, please?" I requested.

After all, wasn't a donation of Kohinoor enough?

The place was gigantic, with every corner stuffed with Britain's history of kings, queens, royal beasts, paintings, jewels, weapons, and much more.

"This will take us forever if we go and study their history. I don't waste time if it is not meant for the exam. Let's skip all this and let's run where the Kohinoor is. Also, these Kings with their history are not as impressive as ours. I am just fascinated by the monstrous size of crows in that cage." Gowardhan was bored and wanted directly to jump on the business.

"Yes, I too feel so. Let's march towards Kohinoor." I agreed.

"Jewels are towards the left, see the signboard."

"Let's start. And, those are not large crows, they are Ravens." I rectified.

'No cameras allowed.' The instruction read on the door of the jewels section.

"Oh, damn! What do they think? Are they afraid-Chinese will take pictures of jewels and design duplicates and conquer the market? Who'll wear these jewels, these days anyway?" Gowardhan buzzed, keeping his DSLR inside.

To our surprise, there was no particular treatment for Kohinoor. This extraordinary diamond was kept along with other ordinary diamonds. There was a conveyor belt for the visitors to stand upon and be the beholder of glittering ornaments, crowns, thrones for which many had let their blood out.

The great moment to witness the pride of India was nearer. My accelerating heart was about to explode. The excitement was at par. We stood on the belt. The belt started rolling out, one by one the chamber of jewels with its brief history was in front of our eyes. Alas! The last one was Kohinoor. In an utter commotion, we forgot to read the short history and just looked at the crown devised with the treasured diamond. We were victorious. We were jubilant. We witnessed the Kohinoor.

"Again" we both shouted towards each other, and went back at the start of the conveyor belt and repeated this thrice.

"That was fulfilling. But frankly, I don't understand what is so special about Kohinoor. Do you?" I humbly asked.

"You don't have artistic eyes, my friend." My friend consoled my poor vision.

On the return journey, in a bus, Gowardhan argued- "But, why was Kohinoor fitted in the cramped spot on the top in the crown I don't understand."

"Wait. It was in the middle." I denied.

"What rubbish! It was at the top. What did you see then?"

"No. It was in the middle. The top one was also a diamond, but not Kohinoor."

"No way. Why is the topmost precious diamond kept in the middle?"

"I'm not the designer with the artistic eyes, but I'm damn sure, it was not on the top."

Throughout the journey, we didn't say anything about Kohinoor. We were thinking for a long time with all our logical senses stretched to find out only one answer- Which diamond was the Kohinoor on the crown?

"Okay," I invaded the silence. "Let's keep this only between us, till further interrogation."

"Deal. The last person to know about this confusion of ours is Varma. Okay?"

"Deal."

***

I surfed all over the internet for the things that should not be done in the UK, particularly London. The first thing came out as not to stand to the left on the escalators. People in a hurry use these escalators not as escalators but as treadmills. In the rush hours, these escalators at the tube stations are used as running tracks. So, it is an interesting scene where one escalator is partitioned into two - one for standing, another one for running.

The next thing to abandon in the UK as per the research was - visiting Madame Tussauds. We grew up reading the news about Madame Tussauds. We grew up watching news of Indian actors inaugurating their statues at that place. Even though we didn't know how to pronounce Madame Tussauds, it is an unwritten rule for tourists to visit Madame Tussauds. If you don't show your weird poses standing beside hot actresses, you are not believed to have travelled to London. The experienced people, especially Brits, don't like this place much. In their opinion, first of all, it's highly expensive. You can imagine if the British claimed it as expensive, how expensive it must be for us. Next, people claim it to be highly crowded. For this point, we can ignore them because Brits don't know what 'crowded' means. I want them to visit Kurla station at 9 am to have a better understanding of the word 'crowded.' With a strong social obligation in mind, even though we knew this place wouldn't be worthy enough of our soft earned money, we decided to visit it to regret it later. But this disappointment of losing money for unworthy activity was anytime better than the regret of not visiting and agitating it later. FOMO dominates.

"Anyways, I didn't change my profile picture in a week." Gowardhan was preparing his mind for the shock of spending a vast amount of money. This guy uses his Facebook account to dump all the pictures we click. Who uploads 78 photos of the house? Answer- Gowardhan aka Gowd on Facebook.

People are crazy about being clicked every time and all the time. These tourist places in London captured this human psychology very well. Wherever we visited a tourist place, there were photo booths. They will click your picture for free of cost. At the exit, you can see your well-photoshopped image with sharks or on the moon or on Harry Potter's broom which lures you to buy the picture at an extraordinarily high cost. Well played Brits. I don't have a problem getting clicked for free when a cute white girl asks you softly. What my problem is, then the same white cute girl asks you to try different awkward poses - like you are giving a flying kiss or as if you are hugging someone or you are falling from the top floor of the Burj Khalifa. I could not pose satisfactorily for any of those due to my inexperience; still posing for the last one was better among the three.

The museum was huge. It was full of glittering lights, camera flashes, and happy people. People were confused where to pose, how to pose, against whom, how many clicks to take and what to do to look abnormal. As soon as we entered, Bollywood stars welcomed us. These stars were groped by Indians only. But as Indians are in huge numbers as always, the block was densely packed. Men were holding a hand of Katrina, some were giving a flying kiss to Aishwarya, and few were clicking sanskari selfies with Madhuri.

"And they say, Indian actresses are looked down upon. See here!" Gowardhan said looking at the scarcity of interest near male actors and jam-packed enthusiasm nearby Katrina-Aishwarya.

You have to be shameless at Madame Tussauds. You need to pose a duck face, puppy face, hold the heroine's hand as if she is your girlfriend and click. The most important thing to do at the museum is getting clicked. Doesn't matter with whom, whether you know the person and regardless of whether the pose suits you. Following the tradition, we too clicked hundreds of weird pictures. They are never visited till date.

"I hate this gender-bias. Just look at that girl. She has inserted her hand in Hrithik's underwear. Where is the decency? And people claim - men are dogs, lecherous and what not. I want to see some feminist's reaction if I go and grab some sculpture's curves. I'll be called by all the names - misogyny, disgusting, disrespectful, lascivious bastard, and whatever synonyms they know.

They talk of feminism forgetting common sense." Gowardhan was in his non-stop express.

Gowardhan needs to revisit the concept of feminism I thought. Before I could say something, he started his engine again. I saw fumes in his eyes.

"One thing you tell me - why do these feminists have great control over English? In a debate, they tend to talk furiously at lightning speed which gives so little time for anyone to think and react sensibly. You tell me-do you know when to use literally and figuratively? You don't, I know. Do you know why many debates are won by feminists? Because they are good at English." He continued tickling Scarlett Johnson's belly.

"But feminism does not mean-" I interrupted only to regret later.

"Okay, okay. Stop. Let's go there. Now, see how I pose and what I grab. You hold the camera tight. Don't shake it. If my picture gets blurred, see what I shake yours", determined Gowardhan summoned. Next two hours Gowardhan posed so strangely that it became so awkward and embarrassing for me to roam as his photographer. We two were looking like those Mumbai Local train Romeos who pose leaning at the door with Ray-Banned goggles and leather jackets in the hot summer.

"You click. Don't be shy." "Come here we will click a selfie." "Who is watching us here anyway?" "No one is looking at you." "You click! Click!!" Gowardhan lured me for pictures with these wordings, and I fell for it, every single time.

Sometimes I wonder how would I live knowing no-one is looking at me? Has it been different than now? Better maybe?

Of course, a thousand times yes.

If you want to prove you are a die-hard academician, you need to visit the temple of knowledge. There are two such renowned temples around London- Oxford and Cambridge. There are deluxe bus and train services for this pilgrimage journey. We chose the bus.

Londoners have a soft corner for students. Not only UK students, but from any part of the world. These students are provided with hefty discounts on bus tickets for visiting these universities.

We were on our way to Oxford.

"These are your tickets. Thank you." greeted the ticket collector at the bus station.

Those were the discounted student tickets. I gave a 'shut-up-and-don't-be-surprised' look to Gowardhan. He reverted the same. I handed over the money and collected the tickets. We were not students. We were not liars either. We didn't tell the truth doesn't make us liars. Everything is fair in love, war and discounted trips.

"With our body built, I don't think we have any problem for another five years to look like a student." I dodged Gowardhan taking the window seat.

"Yes. And we owe that discount. Aren't we students of life?"

The green countryside along the way was looking more beautiful in the presence of soft rain. The lush green farms with an adorable troop of sheep were mesmerising. The bus reached Oxford town precisely on time. Oxford is not just a university; it's a town of exactly the same looking buildings.

"It looks like an architect just copy pasted all the buildings. Or the town has purchased everything in bulk." Gowardhan commented.

We explored tourist spots one by one. Then, we started with the universities. There are a lot of universities, which comes under the hood of Oxford. Their taxonomy is different. In India, we have colleges or institutes which comprises a university, but theirs is a different scene.

"So, it seems anything in this town can be termed as Oxford University. Isn't that funny?" Gowardhan realised.

"So, it seems we are fools if we thought Oxford is just one university."

Same is the case with Cambridge. It is again a town like Oxford and not just a university. Cambridge University is blessed with a river Cam in the middle. There is an exciting activity called punting, a tour in a small boat, to be involved in. A punter acting as a chauffeur will guide you to the colleges located on the banks of the shallow river and inform about the interesting past and alumni.

"Hi! My name is Laura, and I'm your punter." A beautiful young girl welcomed us.

Gowardhan couldn't control his giggle.

"What happened?" I asked.

"Her name," he replied. I too couldn't control my giggle then.

She started with the history of Cambridge and their famous alumni.

"Does anyone know anyone from Cambridge?" She asked for breaking the ice.

"Newton." The whole boat screamed.

"Great. So, this is where Newton used to study and research. All the gravitation theories emerged from here." She pointed to Trinity College pushing the punt against the river bed with a pole. She was again, a beauty with power.

"Was it fortunate or unfortunate?" She laughed.

She continued informing us about the other colleges, their rivalries, their funny incidents with the constant high enthusiasm. She must be exhausted by riding all of us, but she never let her zeal fall anytime.

"But why don't we see students around?" Gowardhan asked suddenly. It was indeed a valid question.

If you visit any academic institution in India, it is full of students. You see nothing but people all around. But the UK case was different. Their universities were scarce.

Universities without students are like ATMs without cash.

"They must be studying." Laura replied with a big grin with 'don't-ask-such-questions' expressions. "They study hard you must be knowing." She continued sarcastically.

"Hey, these all are ancient universities, don't they?" He threw another question.

"Yes, they are. Many of them are from the fifteenth century."

"But do you know which the first university in the world is?"

There was a big question mark on her face.

"Takshashila. From India." Gowardhan said with a bulged chest.

***

"I heard a word or two about IITs. The striving competition and craze about it. Is it a reality?" Harry asked us one day out of the blue.

"Yes, definitely a reality," Gowardhan replied. "If you want a simplified version I can say - Oxford and Cambridge are IITs of Britain."

Varma coughed the water listening to the arguably exaggerated, unprecedented explanation of IITs.

***

The things when repeated gets bored. The same happens when you are on a long-term vacation. You see a garden. You adore it. You love it. After a few days, you visit another one. You love it too. Next few days, lots of them. Now, the garden doesn't feel exciting. It is just like the one you visited some days back. Now, you see gardens only because people say they are famous and you want to tick your visited list. Same happened after spending straight six weekends on sight-seeing.

London is overfilled with museums. We spent the entire day at the first museum. But then others looked similar. There were more free entry museums than free entry toilets in the city. The best part about these museums was there were lavish toilets. So, no old painting or ancient stones attracted us, but the toilets of the museums. 'Pee for free' was our motto.

"So, how many museums did you visit?" One artist friend asked.

"Umm, two we explored and at least ten we peed into," I replied shamelessly.

After visiting the prioritised places from our wish list, our exhilaration stagnated. Our energy levels went down. Enthusiasm dropped. Now, the tourist places were just boxes on the checklist we needed to check.

***

"Listen, comrades." Major Gowardhan was addressing on a moonlit Friday night. "We have limited time and unlimited places to visit. So, we need to prioritise. The important places we have already covered. And thus, fulfilled the social obligation. And frankly, we all know, the remaining places would not be significantly different. So, just take a look, don't go in detail about the place and move forward to the next. Time is money and the ticket prices are high. Click a picture and go to the next." Major declared the plan.

"Now you'll understand the role of a manager. How he has to optimise the resources and prioritise the work. How he can't let go of all the resources all at once - I mean granting Diwali leaves to all." Manager aspirant Mr Sitharaman was going off the track.

"Sleep tight. Wake up early. Good night." Major left, ignoring the endeavouring manager's lesson.

***

When you imagine London, it is incomplete without the stunning London Eye. The giant Ferris wheel on the bank of the Thames is a huge structure more beautiful than its pictures. It tours you the whole and sole of London.

People are crazy. They want to preserve the moments instead of living the moments.

"Look at that beautiful, breath-taking view." My eye was on Big Ben. "And look at those posing for a picture." My other eye was on the people taking pictures keeping Big Ben in the background.

"Does this make sense for people to shoot the video and watch a recorded version later instead of living it in the present?" I asked Gowardhan who was adjusting the lens.

"Who are you to decide for them?" He retorted.

"No, I mean if they can see it live, why record?"

"If they are happy with recordings, let them record. Everyone enjoys it differently. Everyone has their own definition of happiness and their way to pursue that. We can't impose our choices on others."

That day Gowardhan taught me a valuable lesson for life.

***

"Do you know during the second world war, all venomous animals in this zoo were killed?" Varma informed clicking Viper at the London zoo. "To save the chaos and danger in case these animals escape due to the outbreak of bombing."

"Interesting." I appreciated the information.

"Were there no animal activists then?" Gowardhan questioned.

"No idea. Or maybe that event initiated the need for animal activists. But I'm not sure."

The London Zoo is a home for animals all around the world. But Indian Lions and Tigers steal the show. Penguins are provided with a separate beach for themselves while hundreds of other species struggle to mark their presence felt.

"Honey, please hurry up. Look at that gentleman, he too wants to see the tiger, right?" a lady smiling at me asked her little daughter to move aside. I sheepishly smiled back and nodded, appreciating the kind words. I was flattered. 'Gentleman' was the word. That's where Brits melt your heart. What was the need for calling me a gentleman? She could simply ask her daughter to move aside, but she chose to let me feel better, and that's the quality to acquaint from them. Often making others feel better is a free service with minimal effort.

"It's huge. Even if you just glance at the animal and move forward, you won't complete in a day. It's huge." Varma was impressed with the zoo. "I've seen

Penguins, Kangaroos, Lemurs, Giraffes, and many others for the first time." he continued.

"Hey, we too have Giraffes in our Mysore zoo," I informed.

"Yes, and taller than these Giraffes." Gowardhan magnified.

***

"Their life seems so mysterious to me," I whispered, watching the guard-change parade at Buckingham Palace.

"Yes, me too," Gowardhan admitted.

"See, I don't understand their job. Just be here all the time and watch the crowd at the gate."

"No, they frequently are on tours, meeting VIPs, strengthening diplomatic relations and all."

"Wait, about whom you are talking about?" I asked.

"Royal families."

"I'm talking about the royal guards."

"Oh, royal guards? Yes, their job is puzzling. First of all, they stand like statues, and I guess they are there just for the namesake. Police take charge in case of an emergency. So, what do these guards do?"

"Probably for continuing the tradition."

"If you ask me about the job where you get money for not doing anything- I'll say the best one is of royal guards." Gowardhan imagined.

"But you know- not doing anything is tough."

"As in?"

"If you want to scratch, you shall not do anything and stand still. If you want to laugh at people's idiocy, you shall not do anything and stand still. Doing nothing is harder than doing something."

***

"I envy this city. One of the most gifted cities in the world." Gratified Varma announced cautiously watching the opening of the Tower Bridge for the Cruse. "It has everything. Beautiful monuments, lovely disciplined people, cleanliness, different cultures, peace, nightlife. Everything." He extended.

"Just one thing it misses." Gowardhan objected.

"What is that? Poverty?"

"Sea."

"Why do you need a sea? To submerge idols?"

"No, not just for that. To have a peaceful, harmonious public monument on the seashore. A necklace of the city. A shrine to put all your stress in."

"So, are you comparing Marine Drive with these masterpieces?"

"No, I'm not. Marine Drive is incomparable."

Poka Poka

Our trolleys looked so small in front of the huge pile of luggage to be carried over. Still, with a lot of intelligence and space optimised algorithms, we managed to thrust those mountains into the trolleys. If you are good at Tetris, you are good with packing the bags. Our smart techniques included t-shirts rolled inside the jar which mother forced us to carry along, every space-consuming layer of packing from the gifts were torn apart, sister's handbag was filled with socks and towels so no damn air could claim its presence. It was hard to believe the whole luggage was inside those tiny looking trolleys.

"Look at my bag. It's so efficiently packed that if you dip it into the water, you won't see any air bubbles emerging." Gowardhan claimed.

"Let's check. Let's dip it in the tub." Varma ridiculed as a routine.

"I'm worried about its weight now. I hope it's within the limit. Do we have a weighing machine in the house?" Gowardhan ignored Varma's comments and moved on to his next concern.

"I didn't see that anywhere but it must be somewhere. After all, it is a health-conscious people's house." I suspected.

"Or Varma could help me with this. Without the machine, we can guess."

"How?" Confused Varma asked.

"It's simple. Lift me. And then put me down and lift my baggage. If you feel half the stress in the latter case, then it's within the limit." Gowardhan came up with absurd logic.

"What bullshit. Are you really from IIT?"

It was difficult to say goodbye to London. It was hard to bid adieu to the house which was slowly turning out to be our home. The gloomy thoughts of leaving the graceful London after spending a few impish months were making us sad. Apart from the frequent flyer, Mr. Sitharaman, everyone looked blue and down.

"He must be confident enough to come here again." Varma pointed out.

"Maybe." I agreed half-heartedly.

"But, I don't think we can come here again." Gowardhan hopelessly whined watching motionless roads from the window.

"Maybe." I agreed half-heartedly.

"That's the thing. Do you know why leaving London is making us sad and why not our cities when we visit other cities? It is partly because of the memories of the place obviously, but more than that it is because of the thought that we may never revisit the place." Varma was in a different mood.

"Yes, I too think the same. So, it's like we are dull with the anticipation that we may never get to see and talk with these people, never get to travel in tubes, never walk on the roads in such icy weather. Never get to spend busy weekends filled with sightseeing." Gowardhan agreed to Varma. That was rare. First of its kind.

"I understand. I am going to miss this place terribly." Varma emotionally said.

"Yes, me too." I wholeheartedly agreed.

Within a flash of a moment, I witnessed a tight hug of Varma and Gowardhan for the first time. Why does everything get patched up at the end?

***

"Hey guys, make sure you get ready by 4:30. Taxis will be coming on time. Be ready. Don't forget anything here. Don't be late." Mr Sitharaman went into father mode. We followed his instructions. As he stated, the taxis were exactly on time. Brits never gave us a chance to crib about their particularity of time. Two black taxis with their white drivers were waiting outside our home.

"Let me handle this, Sir." Both drivers took care of our baggage and delicately put up into the taxies with smiling faces. The mischievous times were flashing in front of my eyes. The lane, nearby signal, exact looking houses in a row, the neighbouring lady with a dog, all, all were appearing familiar by then. Within a minute taxis started one after the other. We hardly got a minute to check out our home, probably for the last time.

Gowardhan and I occupied the first, and the other two were in another taxi.

"Hey, any idea how much time it would take?" I asked the driver.

"It usually takes 45 minutes. But it's quite an early morning, so I suspect not much traffic. We should be there by 30 minutes." He politely answered. "Or 25, as it shows." He pointed out the GPS device. I remembered the Congo driver of the first day. How nice that day was!

The driver turned on the FM. The volume level was perfect. Even though I did not get what song was played on, it was soothing my mind. I was feeling content and wistful at the same time. I looked out of the window. It was dark with some glittering due to car lights. Maybe like us, many people were heading to leave London. My mind slowed down watching the fast-moving cars outside. The flash of moments spent, of all kinds - crazy, funny, silly, was running on my mind and then slowly stopped. The vehicles outside were passing at lightning speed. The precious last few London moments were agile. And there was me, sitting numbly without any thoughts, watching outside, hoping not to reach the destination any sooner. Similar was the condition of Gowardhan sitting beside me, watching another side of the road. There was abyssal silence in the taxi, just FM playing some alien songs. No one was speaking to anyone. I guess, the driver was experienced with such mind turbulence of the people leaving the place for forever. He too was silent and did not disturb our disturbed minds further.

Slowly, the outside dark started gleaming. I suspected the airport nearer. About a minute later, it was full of lights.

"Here you go, Sir." The driver slowly parked the taxi and started helping us to take out the baggage. "Thank you very much, Sir. Have a nice journey ahead and visit us soon." He said and gave us a thin smile.

"Yes, sure. Thank you very much." Optimistic me replied by taking out the handle of the trolley and started my way towards the motherland.

I was not surprised when it took exactly 30 minutes to reach the airport. My belief in intuition got stronger, and technology a bit weaker.

***

29.6 - showed the baggage weighing counter and I took a deep sigh. The baggage of others too was within the limit. We stood in the queue for a security check waiting for our turn watching people going through security checks.

"Sometimes I wish to become an Airport security crew in the western countries." Gowardhan expressed his desire to change his career, observing a young girl take off her jacket.

"That's creepy, man," Varma remarked watching the same young girl.

"I was just joking." Gowardhan lied.

"I'm roaming around the duty-free shops. Anyone want to join?" Mr Sitharaman informed us after our check-in.

"Sure. Let's go." We shouted in unison. Who doesn't love shopping?

My heart was melting seeing the same products which I bought from London significantly cheaper in the airport's duty-free shops. Mr Sitharaman was unstoppable there. He had a detailed list of what to buy, and so he was in full swing.

"I know what you are thinking." Mr Sitharaman said to me.

"What?"

"You are regretting purchasing perfumes from the city. Don't you?"

"Yes. How do you know? And wait, did you buy the same ones?" I glanced in his basket.

"Yes. Didn't you know about the duty-free shops? They are always cheaper than the city outlets."

"Oh, so, why didn't you tell us that earlier?" I was angry at him. After all, it was a matter of money.

"If I had told you, you wouldn't have believed. In fact, on my first visit, I too made the same mistakes as yours. Take experience and learn." Father figure spoke again.

"I understand. But this experience is costly. That's not right. You should have told us. That's not right." I repeated.

Mr Sitharaman went to the billing counter and returned after a minute.

"Okay. Did you buy chocolates?" He asked. I sensed his improved version.

"Few I bought from London for the family, and I know they too must be costlier. Now, I want to buy some more for our colleagues and some for the family." I told him. My buoyant eyes were expecting penny-saving suggestions from him.

"Okay. So, buy chocolates for your family from here. And don't buy any chocolates for our colleagues from here. We will buy them from Mumbai duty-free shops." He suggested.

"Wait. So, the last time when you returned with chocolates, those too were from Mumbai?"

"Of course." Mr Sitharaman shyly smiled.

The biggest crime you can commit while returning from a foreign country is not bringing the chocolates and alcohol. If your luggage misses chocolates and alcohol, the airport security crew will take you aside and can investigate you. You may even be kept behind bars. The sole purpose of your visit was to bring these items for others, isn't it? My friend was abashed for not bringing complete two litres of allowed duty-free alcohol. He brought only one and a half. Some people are born just to snatch everyone's duty-free quota.

I was gawking at the Blue Label when I noticed Gowardhan's cart too had Blue Label.

I buzzed, "You too?" looking at his carry case.

He said, "Yes, Ashutosh wants Blue Label".

"What? Ashutosh asked you too? He asked me too."

Then we asked one another who asked what to bring for them and found out Ashutosh was not the only one. Indians you know, they love to have a backup option.

Chocolates are inevitable. The news of the return is recognised by 'chocolates in the pantry' email. If you don't bring them, you are not socially accepted. People are fooled as they think chocolates are brought from a foreign country. It is hard to control laughter when self-proclaimed foodies claim, "They are fabulous, man. I mean - that's real dark chocolate. In India, you don't get those. Not even 50% of its darkness. I've tried almost all places in India but couldn't find such. London is a hub for that. Thanks, man!"

The flight was on time. The giant Airbus was in front of us. We were saving the last few shots of London in our memories. India was calling. There was no reason to be sad actually. The thoughts of India, family, friends, and food rejoiced my mind. The dullness was replaced by elation. The sadness was killed by excitement. I was feeling happy. It made me happy imagining the happy faces waiting for me in India. Your mind knows how to heal you. Isn't it the one who knows you inside out?

We boarded the flight. We occupied our seats and followed the instructions. The plane took off. I was examining the city for the last time, remembering the time when we landed at the same airport a few months back. That was a pleasant evening, and then it was a luminous early morning we were leaving the city. Everything was the same, except my mind. It was filled with all sorts of UK memories to cherish throughout life. And confident me. At least to place an order perfectly and subtly at Subway.

The sign of the seat-belt went off. It was good to let go off the seat belt, but I was too engrossed in my thoughts looking outside the window. Suddenly someone gently tapped on my shoulders, and it felt like to come out of a captivated dream.

"Sorry, Sir. You can now remove your seat belt and sit comfortably if you wish." An air hostess was advising me cordially. Anyone hardly likes being advised by a stranger, but, who wouldn't, when someone so gracious is so polite in the technique?

"Yes, sure. Thanks for that." I told the Brit lady, while I tried to get rid of the belt by myself. By that time, we were knowledgeable enough to recognize people from their accents.

"What would you like to have Sir? Tea or Coffee?" She asked.

"Of course Tea," I replied in a little time.

Suddenly I remembered Brit's biscuit coloured tasteless tea.

"Oh sorry, Coffee please." I changed my choice the next moment.

She smiled as a part of her job. It reminded me of Eva.

"Here it is. And here is your sandwich." She served the coffee and chicken sandwich.

"Hey, I'm a vegetarian. Give me a vegetarian option, please."

During my whole stay nothing could convert me to non-vegetarian. I was not frail enough to break down in front of the Brit beauty and her honeyed words.

"Oh, I'm so sorry. But Sir, right now I'm short of veg sandwiches." She made a puppy face. "What I can do is - I'll serve a few, and bring you the veg option if that's okay with you." She continued.

"Yeah, makes sense. By that time, I'll finish my tea." I said.

She raised her eyebrows making herself cuter.

"Oh, sorry I mean - coffee." I corrected myself.

"Sure," she said and widely smiled. I could see the geniality on her happy smile. I'm not sure till this day whether that was because I said, 'makes sense' to her or whether I accepted to wait. But, as far as I know Brits, I bet on the former one.

Finishing coffee, I was about to take a nap when again I felt the familiar gentle tap on my shoulders. My sluggish eyes met her sparkling eyes again.

"Here it is, Sir. Thank you." She handed me the packet and left smiling.

With a veg sandwich, there was an additional surprise- a pineapple pastry. I guess my remark of 'makes sense' had shown its charm.

Epilogue

The Airbus arrived at Mumbai airport quite smoothly. As soon as the tyres touched the ground, people stood up hovering over neighbours to get their luggage before others and ran.

"Thank God, at least the runway is pothole free." Varma chuckled watching futile attempts of passengers creating turmoil. "Just look at there." he continued, pointing at the unordered crowd inside the plane.

"That's excitement." Gowardhan was justifying the act.

I was happy. I was going home after a long time. My Indian tea was waiting for me at home. My loved ones were waiting for their gifts at home. I was in my thoughts which brought a smile on my face which remained throughout baggage collection and security check. When Gowardhan was busy buying the chocolates, disinterested I was standing outside, still in my thoughts. Out of the UK habit, I unknowingly and by accident smiled at a young stranger Indian girl.

She looked surprised. She looked irked. She stared at me hard. She whispered something in her friend's ear. She too stared at me. Harder.

"Hurry up and call the taxi now," I ordered Gowardhan. I was frightened. I was hasty. Taxi arrived. I jumped into it. I looked back. She was seen nowhere in my visibility. I sighed. After all, who likes to get arrested?

About the Author

Sandeep is a proud alumnus of IIT Bombay. Being an IITian, he is obliged to write something, and coincidentally he likes to write. Besides writing, he loves to dance when no one is shooting, do stand-up comedy when everyone promises to laugh and travel abroad when someone else is paying. He is a keen observer, and that reflects in his writing.

Currently, he lives in Pune and works in a software company for a living. Previously, he worked in Gurgaon, Mumbai, Bangalore and of course London. He is accustomed to industry's rituals and practices and thus has given himself a license to reveal its secrets for all.

Sandeep is a morning tea person. He makes beautiful tea daily exclusively for himself and drinks it too!

Also from the Author

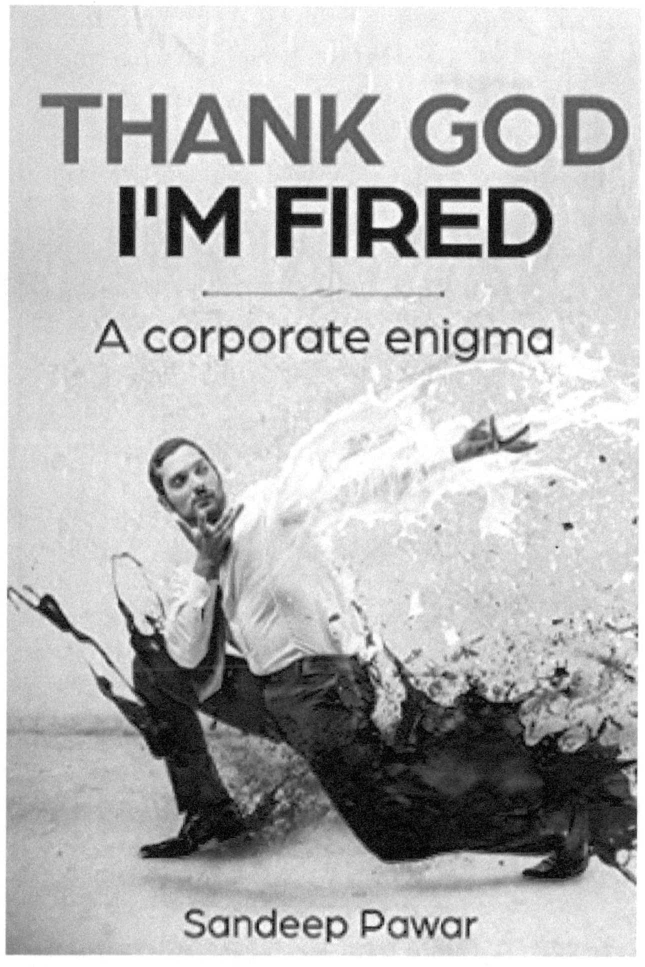

Thank God I'm Fired

What do you do when you think you are trapped in the wrong job? Leave the job and do what you love. Simple, isn't it? But what if you neither have the guts to leave the job nor know what you love to do? Complicated, isn't it?

Meet Raghav, who like millions of other software professionals, is stuck in a similar situation. But don't worry, his destiny has better plans for him. What plans you may ask? Well, getting him fired.

This novella takes you on a light-hearted tour of the contemporary software industry where you can ask the haunting question loudly - is getting sacked a blessing in disguise?